Her Picture-Perfect Family

LINDA BARRETT

DEDICATION

To my readers --

Without you, the books are unfinished.

I'd be talking to myself.

Thank you for not letting that happen!

Cover art by Rogenna Brewer

www.sweettoheat.blogspot.com

E-book and print formatting by Web Crafters

www.webcraftersdesign.com

Copy Editing by Amy Knupp

www.blueotterediting.com

CHAPTER ONE

When he heard the quick footsteps heading toward his office, Bartholomew Quinn rose from his comfortable leather chair, eager to meet his visitor. His knee ached with the effort. "Don't have time for the arthritis," he mumbled, limping across the room, "no matter how many years behind me. And blast this weather for causing it." Opening the door, he glanced at the petite young woman on the threshold. He grinned with delight and forgot about his pain.

Rain dripped from the hood of her bright red jacket. A red umbrella— closed and dry—hung from her wrist next to a large, colorful tote bag. His gaze drifted lower. She wore sandals; her feet were soaked. "Ach, lassie, come in, come in. You're wet through and through."

"But I'm right on time," she announced, cocking her head. "Aren't I?"

Quinn's laughter fed his soul while filling the room. "That you are, my girl. That you are." The kindergarten teacher had become a favorite of everyone in Pilgrim Cove. Quite an accomplishment in only two years. From the beginning, Bart thought she seemed barely older than her young charges. He wasn't alone in that, but she had the knack of the classroom, of making each child feel special, which, in his opinion, was the secret of her success.

"You're not only on time, Joyful MacKenzie, but a sight for sore eyes, too. So, let's get you dry."

She hung her jacket over a hook on the coat stand and shook out her hair. Short, blonde, and feathery. "Will winter come early, I wonder? It's almost Labor Day, and school's starting within the week. We simply cannot build snow people before we pick apples in the orchard. Well…I suppose we can, but that's topsy-turvy."

Bart understood that by "we," she meant her class. If there was an adventure to be had for the children, Joy was in the middle of it. The parents loved her for it and helped out.

"Always autumn before winter. That's the way of it," said Bart. "You'll pick those apples soon." He gestured to the visitor's chair in front of his desk. "Make yourself comfortable." He watched as she tucked one foot under her bottom and sat.

In his own chair now, he leaned forward. "So how can Quinn Real Estate and Property Management help you?"

She dug into her tote bag. "It's the strangest thing," she said, pulling out an envelope. "I've been evicted. Thrown out. Mrs. Williams needs my apartment for her newly married daughter." She handed the letter to him.

He perused the correspondence. It didn't take long. "The note's dated a month ago. Why didn't…? Ahh—

now I remember. You've been away visiting your family on Cape Cod."

For one fraction of a second, her blue eyes darkened; a shadow hovered. "That's right. I was on vacation. In Provincetown. I forgot to forward the mail, and it…I don't know…I guess it just piled up."

Something was amiss. Sooner or later, Bart would find out what—he took pride in keeping up with all of Pilgrim Cove's residents—but the wee gal needed help now. And he was the one who could solve her problem.

"Rent or buy?" he asked.

"Oh…I wish I could buy. I love this town so much, I'd live here forever. But even I know what's possible and impossible." She leaned over the desk. "Mr. Quinn, a teacher doesn't earn a king's ransom, but I love my work so much I sometimes wonder if I should pay the school board instead of them paying me for being with the children."

"Joy Mackenzie!" he exclaimed, banging his fist on the desk. "Loving your profession is no small thing. We need more like you in our schools. Not that Pilgrim Cove has bad schools, no sirree. High school scores are soaring since Rachel Levine came back to town."

Joy nodded. "We have a pretty strong staff on all levels." She took his hand. "My folks would love me to move back to Provincetown. They're getting more vocal about it, especially since this eviction came up. So can you work some magic and find me a home right away?"

He didn't know much about her folks, some artsy people, he'd heard, but it seemed Joy would certainly rather stay put in Pilgrim Cove.

"So, it's magic you want? Well, not to worry. The house I'm thinking of comes with its own built-in magic. But it's only temporary, mind you, until we find you a new place to hang your hat."

"With school starting next week, I just need some breathing room. A couple of months will be fine. So where will it be?"

"You'll have a view of the ocean, the cry of the gulls, and a beachfront you can't normally afford. Sea View House is the place for you. The upstairs apartment is available, and the price is right."

He named a low figure, and her mouth fell open. "It's part of the William Adams Foundation," he explained. "He was a cousin of John Adams, our second president, you know. And it's leased on a sliding scale. Perhaps you can save some money while you're there…?" Hint. Hint. He wondered at the lack of financial literacy with some young people.

She beamed. "Great idea. Thank you very much. I know where it is, on Beach Street. Everyone in Pilgrim Cove knows about Sea View House."

"But no one knows exactly how it operates, except for the ROMEOs. And we don't talk."

She put both feet down and leaned back in her chair. A smile broke out. "Ahh—Mr. Quinn, the ROMEOs. Retired Old Men Eating Out. However, you're not retired or old. But you're a man for sure. And with your daughters in the restaurant business, you probably do eat out a lot. For that, I don't blame you. Not at all."

Clever. Clever. His band of brothers couldn't have been described more succinctly than Joyful MacKenzie had done. Right on the money, too.

"I count myself lucky to be your tenant," said Joy.

"Good. Good. There's just one more thing."

Her brow furrowed for a second. "Whatever it is, I can handle it."

"While you're living in the Crow's Nest upstairs, there will be another tenant downstairs in the Captain's Quarters. Separate entrances, of course."

Her quick smile returned. "That's even better. I'll enjoy the company. My mom says I've never met a person I didn't like. So what's her name?"

"Not her. *Him*. His name is Logan Nash. He's already moved in." Quinn's thoughts spun like scenes in a kaleidoscope. He hadn't planned this one in advance, but he'd take advantage of what fell into his lap. He had an oversupply of those gut feelings people talked about. And those feelings were bubbling up right now. Joy MacKenzie would be perfect for the troubled photographer.

He rubbed his hands together in anticipation. Autumn was about to begin in Pilgrim Cove. He knew the magic would begin again, too.

Logan Nash stood at the water's edge, face lifted to the ominous gray sky. "Come on, come on! Open up and let 'er rip."

The saturated clouds responded to his plea, and his laughter ping-ponged through the heavy drops. Alone on the beach, Logan spread his arms wide, shook his head, his shaggy mane now soaked through to his scalp. Cool and wet rain—he loved it. Such a relief from the hot, dry winds of Iraq and the heat of the Afghan summer. He'd been embedded with the U.S. military twice, and twice was enough.

His body clenched. His lids shut tight. *Forget about it. Not your problem anymore.* His goal right now was to rest and recover. An R and R just like real soldiers needed. An easy prescription to write, but not so easy to implement. Although he'd produced good stories during the past two years, he wanted to forget everything else about that time. He needed to focus on the future.

He was relieved to be on his own now. Pilgrim Cove, a peninsula snuggled between the Atlantic Ocean and Pilgrim Bay, provided an environment completely different from the one he'd left behind in the Mideast. Renting a house at the beach seemed a good choice, especially since he'd sub-let his small condo in Boston.

And Sea View House had elbow room! Plenty of privacy, too. He'd be able to doodle and noodle and play around with a bunch of ideas for new projects. Looking ahead was the key.

Lightning flashed, and he started jogging toward the big gray house. His wet shirt clung to his skin; his khaki shorts would need days to dry. When thunder boomed, his heart lurched; his muscles tensed. He forced himself not to drop in place to the ground. Instead, he sprinted toward the house. After reaching the back porch, he collapsed onto a redwood chair. He trembled, from head to foot, inside and out.

"Idiot! No bombs. No landmines. Just Thor with his bowling balls." Yeah. Yeah. That's all. A story. Relax.

"Thor? Why, I love Greek mythology, too."

He jumped and twirled. The voice came from another wooden chair not five feet away. From a child in a red raincoat, the hood framing a sweet face. He kept his distance.

"Are you lost? Does your mother know you're here?" His raspy voice reminded him that he'd barely spoken all day. No phone calls. No people in his face. Just the way he liked it. He cleared his throat.

"M-my mother? Lost?" The girl grinned and then laughed as though he'd told a very good joke. "I'm sorry, Mr. Nash, but I seem to have the advantage." She rose and walked closer, arm extended. "I'm your new upstairs neighbor, Joy MacKenzie."

He stood but ignored her gesture. "Quinn didn't say anything about renting out the Crow's Nest."

6

She looked at her empty hand, tilted her head back until her eyes met his. "Did I catch you at a bad time?"

Her meaning was obvious, but he wasn't worried about etiquette, niceties, or putting on a show. He wanted his privacy. Which was why he'd jumped at renting Sea View House. No neighbors on either side after the season, which ended this weekend on Labor Day. And Bart Quinn had said the apartment upstairs was empty.

"Any time would be a bad time. You should find somewhere else to live." He headed into the house. "I've got to make a call."

He found Bart's business card, actually a ROMEO business card, listing all the names, numbers, professional skills, and services of Bart's buddies. The old man was at the top of the list, and he answered on the first ring.

"So you've met the wee lass, have ya? Good, good. She needs a place right now, with school starting in a week and her apartment gone."

"I don't need a neighbor."

"Ach, my boy. You don't know that at all, do you? But I can tell you this: in Pilgrim Cove, we take care of our own…"

He was screwed. The girl must be a native.

"…and now that includes you. So be nice to the wee gal, Logan Nash. At least until I find her a new home."

In a small town like Pilgrim Cove, how many places could there be? "So, not too long then, Mr. Quinn?"

"As long as it takes. It's got to be just right. She's special. Just like you." The old man rang off, and Logan stared at his quiet cell phone. *Just like you?* More than simply leasing Sea View House to him, Quinn viewed

Logan as part of the entire community—whether he wanted to be or not.

Screwed again.

##

The rain had lessened by the time Logan returned outside. The girl was gone, however, and he rolled his shoulders, feeling the tightness ease. A reprieve.

Until he heard a door slam and a female voice call, "Sorry." He walked to the far end of the porch, leaned over the rail, and turned toward the noise. Halfway down the side of the building was another door, which he'd ignored in the three days he'd been there. Ignored until now. When he'd come here with Bart Quinn, the man had mentioned a second entrance leading to the vacant upstairs apartment. An unimportant fact to Logan at the time.

He sighed and gazed back toward the mighty Atlantic, now covered in a gray haze. The ocean had mesmerized and soothed him every day he'd been there. He'd listened to the waves hitting the shore one after the other in a rhythm that continued until the tide changed. The white noise had become an ever-present companion. The unique aroma of seaweed, salt, and ocean did the same. He'd inhaled until his lungs could hold no more. A delicious fragrance. All worth the inconvenience of a neighbor.

He wouldn't leave the beach house. Certainly not on account of a "wee gal." The Quinn guy was a character. A curmudgeon. Logan would assess the situation and handle it, his MO since he was a kid. Simply ignoring the girl might do the trick. Survival depended on sharp eyes, a sharp brain, great flexibility, and trusting no one.

The door slammed once more. The red raincoat appeared as the girl stepped outside.

"Sorry again for the noise. I'll figure something else out by tomorrow…unless you want to be the door monitor…?" She grinned.

A nanosecond flew by.

"Oh, don't look so grumpy," she said. "I was only kidding. I'll use a chair or carton—or something—when I bring my stuff."

"You won't have to," he said, pointing to a spot on the siding. "If you insert the hook from the screen door into that eye, it will stay open for you. I imagine the inside door is not spring weighted. You won't have a problem there."

She stared at the simple arrangement and beamed up at him. "Isn't that clever? I never noticed. Thanks."

He turned to go.

"Oh, one more thing," she said.

He pivoted.

"You're not painting the place or anything, are you? I've got a parakeet, and the fumes would"—she took a step closer to him—"be lethal." She whispered the final words as though the bird could hear and understand. Was she not playing with a full deck?

"Your parakeet's safe. No plans to paint."

Her smile almost blinded him. Talk about lethal. "That's so good to know, Logan. Thanks. I want Happy to be safe in his new home."

"Happy?"

"That's his name. And it's perfect. He's a lovely bird; we talk all the time."

That—he could believe. "You're a good match. A magpie and a parakeet."

She seemed to grow an inch taller. "I don't insult easily, Logan Nash. Better a chirping magpie than a lone wolf howling at the night."

Was that how she saw him? She was on to something but hadn't gotten it quite right. Not a wolf but a German shepherd. Ajax was still part of the military's K-9 Corps but ready to be retired. Tomorrow's appointment at Hanscom Air Force Base had been set up almost a month ago. The shepherd would be coming home with him. Pets were welcome at Sea View House. He'd checked that out with Quinn before seeing the place.

Logan's petite neighbor, however, had struck a chord. Lone wolf. "You know nothing about me, Ms. MacKenzie. Nor is there a need to know."

Ajax was not her business. Inside Logan's camera were dozens of pictures of Tommy Rutherford, the young Marine handler and his four-legged partner. Inseparable—except by death. And Logan had been there from the beginning, arriving at the overseas base the same day as Tommy and his dog.

He already had a dog bed in his SUV and at Sea View House. He had prepared a long checklist of medical topics to discuss with the military vet. He'd bought a leash and collar and a couple of "big dog" toys. Logan was ready to reunite with Ajax.

The magpie spoke up. "We're sharing a house, Mr. Nash. It will be difficult to remain strangers."

"We share a building, Ms. MacKenzie. That's all it is. A big, gray, clapboard-sided building. With two separate doors for our two separate lives. Remaining apart won't be difficult at all."

He did an about-face and headed toward his kitchen, ignoring the laughter his last remark had provoked. The girl was clueless. A parakeet. A butterfly. Flitting here. Flying there. Depending on others to get her out of a jam. Bart had said something about school starting soon. Was she a teacher? Good Lord, the kids probably walked all over her.

He grabbed one of his Nikons and headed to the shoreline. What would a storm leave behind on the beach? With his camera in hand, he'd not only satisfy his curiosity but also find his equilibrium again. A little girl in a red raincoat was not going to throw him off balance.

CHAPTER TWO

The sun shone on Joy's moving day as though the earlier storms had never occurred. She moved from one room to another, making mental notes about her "stuff" — where to put what. *Sea View House might be temporary, but it's going to be my home.* She tossed several colorful accent pillows onto the bench seat along the kitchen wall and sighed. A first step.

When she finally bought her own place, she'd scout flea markets and secondhand stores to find just the right pieces with the right flavor. Unique pieces that she'd love. A forever place needed her own style.

In the meantime, the apartment at Sea View House would do very well. Two nice bedrooms provided space for sleeping, as well as for craftwork and lesson prep, while a spacious country kitchen and sitting room combo provided elbow room for living. Lots of cabinets and closets were tucked everywhere. The delightful bonus, however, was the wood-planked deck, just outside the kitchen, that stretched the width of the house. She wondered how she'd get anything done when views of the Atlantic pulled her as strongly as any tide.

By late afternoon, however, she'd dragged dozens of cartons upstairs, as well as suitcases and tote bags. Her muscles ached; her head ached. Unpacking would have to wait for the next day.

Her mouth tightened as warnings to *take it easy for a while* echoed in her mind. She wasn't in pain anymore, and she was healthy. With impatient hands, she rubbed her eyes and made her way once more to the outside deck. Taking a deep breath, she inhaled the familiar seaside aroma and calmed down instantly. A reminder of home. Of family.

She hadn't seen nor heard her neighbor all day. Maybe he'd lit out on purpose. Maybe he was afraid she'd ask for help with her move. Pooh! He needn't have worried. If she'd wanted help, she could have arranged for it. The ROMEOs would have put out a call for some teens, and she would have tipped them well. She sighed. Who was she kidding? She could have used the extra hands, but now that the heavy work was over, she preferred her privacy.

Tomorrow she'd sort her stuff. Linens. Curtains. Books. Art supplies. Sewing machine. Clothes. Shoes. Teaching syllabus and extra school supplies. Decorative pieces she'd bought and ones she'd made. Canned foods she hadn't used before leaving town. And, most important, her framed photos. Once the family pictures were set in place, the apartment would feel even more like home.

She glanced at the parakeet perched on his swing. The kitchen seemed to be the heart of the apartment, so that was where Joy had set his cage.

"I'm filthy, sweaty, and tired," she said, "but I'm glad you look content." She whistled, waited, and heard his response, then opened the cage door and stroked the soft blue feathers. "Not letting you out today, Happy. We'll wait awhile until you get used to the place."

The budgie cocked his head.

"I wonder why you and your pals are called bird brains," said Joy. "I bet you understand everything I'm saying. Which is more than I can say about the lone wolf downstairs. Not becoming friends when we share a house? Ridiculous."

An image of the absent Logan Nash appeared in her mind's eye. The shaggy dark hair, brilliant gray eyes, broad shoulders. His delineated calf muscles. She'd noticed them. She'd noticed each detail. Her palm itched. Her fingers reached for an imaginary pencil. She had to get him down on paper.

Fatigue forgotten, she rummaged through her art carton until she found what she needed. Then she wondered for the umpteenth time where he'd been.

Logan pulled into the Visitor Control Center parking lot at Hanscom Air Force Base that afternoon, paperwork at his side—driver's license, passport, car insurance, and registration. He'd always known he'd adopt the dog, but now he was surprised at how eager, nervous, and excited he was about seeing Ajax again. How would the dog react to him after being apart for months?

Maybe it wouldn't work. Maybe Logan would remind the shepherd of Tommy too much. Dogs grieved. That was a proven fact. Maybe Jax would mope and whine constantly. Doubts moved in, putting a damper on Logan's expectations.

With the efficiency he'd come to expect when working with the U.S. Military, Logan was taken to the kennel facility. He offered a quick salute to the desk officer. "After spending a long time with the Army, it's become an automatic reflex," he said with a laugh.

"No need to apologize," replied the sergeant. "Here comes Major Johnson, our veterinarian, the man you want to see."

The major came forward, hand extended. "I've read your stories. Mr. Nash. The photos are extraordinary. Excellent job, especially your series about our war dogs. Loved the title, too. Soldiers of a Different Breed. We want the country to know about our four-legged warriors."

"Thank you. Thanks very much. I was honored to be part of such a group." He swallowed hard. "My effort, however, was small—ah, compared to some others."

"Not small, Mr. Nash. You hit the target. From *Parade* magazine to *National Geographic* to the syndicated news services. No, sir, I wouldn't say small."

Logan's ears burned. He looked down at his feet, then over the man's shoulder. He kept a file of his clippings—electronic and print—but not the professional reviews. He didn't read any of them. He figured his work either told the story or didn't. Since he wasn't starving, he also figured he and his Nikon did all right.

"Hmm…how's Ajax?" He wiped his damp hands against his slacks.

The major missed nothing. "Everyone's a bit nervous when adoption day comes." He glanced at the sergeant. "Time to get the dog. Put him through his paces." The man saluted and left.

"He's a trainer," said Major Johnson. "Been with Ajax some weeks now. We'll take a look, and then we'll see…"

We'll see? What the…? More hoops. Logan understood he was under surveillance. As he watched Ajax, the major would be watching him. No one was going to turn over a member of the K-9 Corps to him just because Logan had filled out some forms and paid for Ajax's transport to the States.

The actual handlers in the field had first dibs on their dogs, but Tommy wasn't here. Police departments had second dibs. But Ajax was ten years old, too old to warrant more financial investment. The Logan-and-Ajax team was a special case.

"Come on, son" invited the major. "The sergeant's bringing him to the training room. We can watch through the glass—a one-way mirror. You'll be able to hear, too."

His heartbeat quickened again. Finally, he'd see his old friend.

Down one hall and around another until they stood in front of a glass window. The room was empty.

"Ever own a dog before?"

"No, sir." Was that a strike against him? "But I can learn."

The major spoke into a small mic, the kind used by news reporters. "Put him though basic obedience first. Mr. Nash needs to watch, listen, and learn."

So maybe not a strikeout yet.

"Son, you've been with Ajax long enough to appreciate how well trained he is. In civilian life, you want him to remain trained and obedient. Not for sniffing IEDs but for socializing appropriately with friends and community."

"I lead a solitary sort of life," said Logan, "but I see what you mean. Taking him for a walk…"

The vet nodded. "Exactly. Recognizing neighbors. Who belongs and who doesn't. Ownership is a big responsibility."

"Understood." Of course he understood, but theory had given way to reality. His reality.

A door opened into the training room. And there was Ajax. A silver-and-black, broad-chested gorgeous fellow. For a moment, Logan couldn't breathe.

"That's our boy," he said, his voice raspy, his mind flashing back to some rugged Afghanistan terrain. "Thank you. Thank you for taking such good care of him. He's been through hell."

"I understand you were right there in hell with him. Isn't that so?"

"I…suppose, but…I-I managed." Usually by not getting involved. This experience had been different, but he kept that thought to himself.

He watched and listened to the trainer as he put Ajax through the basic commands. Sit. Stay. Down. Heel. Come. Always rewarding the canine with a hug or kibble. Then came the more advanced orders. Stop. Back off. Stand. Drop it. Leave it.

"He hasn't forgotten a thing," said Logan. "He should be the valedictorian of his class."

Johnson chuckled. "Almost every one of our MWDs could take the honor. In fact, with the many thousands of dollars put into their training, they should all have PhDs."

So far, the sergeant had been working with Ajax almost silently, except for the commands and praise words. Soon he changed the routine. He sat down on a chair with the dog seated in front of him and started speaking in a conversational tone.

"I was playing cards with Logan Nash the other day…"

The dog howled as soon as the familiar name was spoken. A full body shiver traveled though Logan. "Where's the door?" he demanded, starting to search.

"Hang on, son." The vet spoke into the mic. The trainer nodded.

"It's time, Mr. Nash. Someone wants to see you again—in the flesh."

He took Logan back around the corner to the door and opened it. The dog was staring at the trainer as he'd

17

been told, his back to Logan. "Stand here," whispered the vet, "and call his name quietly. Then brace yourself."

He had to clear his throat. "Jax—come on, boy."

The dog twirled on two hind legs and bolted for Logan. Slobbering kisses followed. Cries and whines. A lot of licking. More cries. Then he attached himself to Logan's side.

"I missed you too, boy." He hadn't known just how much until that very moment. He wiped his eyes, not caring what the two hardened soldiers thought about his tears.

"It should be Tommy Rutherford picking him up. Not me." Another howl at Tommy's name. Another lick.

Logan rubbed the dog under the neck. "But we'll be okay, right, Jax?" He looked at the men. "I'm renting a place on the beach. Ajax will get as much exercise as he can handle."

"You need a local vet. Ajax has the beginning of arthritis. He's in good shape, but he is ten years old—a mature dog. We'll give you lists of appropriate foods and treats as well as his vaccination dates, but you need someone local you can rely on."

"I've already contacted Adam Fielding in Pilgrim Cove. He came highly recommended." By Bart Quinn, of course. The man knew everyone.

"There's only one more item on our agenda," said the major.

Ah…*this* item he could handle. "I brought my camera," said Logan. "We need to capture Jax's once-in-a-lifetime event."

"Then leash him up, and let's get on with it. Another success story."

They gathered at the flagpole where Private Ajax D.173 was formally retired from the military with appropriate ceremony.

"I'll send a picture to Tommy's grandparents in Maine," said Logan.

"You've seen them?"

He nodded. "They needed to know we were there— Jax and I—and Tommy wasn't alone at the end."

Being alone, however, sounded good to him now. The intense emotions of the day were taking a toll, and he wanted to take Jax and leave.

Major Johnson seemed to recognize Logan's impatience. "Good luck to you, son," he said with a handshake. "And to our boy here." He rubbed the dog's ruff and left.

Ajax danced at Logan's side as they walked to the SUV. "In you go, boy." The dog jumped, found his bed, lay down, and sighed.

Logan laughed out loud. "I feel the same way, buddy." For the first time in a long while, Logan felt the tension leave his body, his muscles as relaxed as deflated balloons. Felt damn good.

He got behind the wheel and revved the engine. "Wait till we get home. You'll love running on the beach right near the water, and you're going to love Sea View House. There's a yard in the back, and a porch. And, oh…I almost forgot. There's a neighbor upstairs."

According to his instructions, he had to introduce Jax to the "community." Which would include Little Red Riding Hood. He glanced at the dashboard clock. "She moved in today—if she stuck to her plan. So we'll have to put up with her for a while. She's much too…too outgoing. Too friendly. And one more thing. She's small, so don't jump on her."

With those words, the need to reinforce Jax's training became a reality. All the commands he'd heard today at the base had to be automatic at all times. He had faith in Ajax. Needed to work on himself.

"But whatever you do, buddy, don't hunt down her parakeet. It's not a toy." He had no doubt she'd let it out of the cage. A butterfly like her…? Didn't seem to have an ounce of common sense.

##

Wrapped in a crocheted blanket and holding a cup of tea, Joy made her way to the wide deck. She stretched out on the lounge chair and watched the moon rise in the night sky. Not a full moon, not till later in the month, but even a quarter moon shed enough light to lure beautiful fairies out to dance on the water. She smiled at her fantasy, then pursed her lips. Grow up! Life wasn't about dreams and fairy tales anymore. Forget about a husband. Forget about children. She'd forge a different dream for herself.

Sipping the tea, she blinked at the brilliant jewels floating on the crest of each ocean wave. That's what moonlight could do. Provide crystals and diamonds free for the asking.

Her muscles ached. After all the packing and schlepping, a sore body was no surprise. She'd earned her respite but had to admit that for a single gal, she'd accumulated a lot of goods. A sewing machine. Hanks of yarn. And clothes. The list never got shorter, but at least she used everything.

In the lounge chair, she snuggled under the afghan of her own making. She'd also designed her larger bedspread in a granny square pattern, using blues, greens, yellow, and black. Her own mother had exclaimed over it. High praise from the noted American stained glass artist Daisy MacKenzie.

Joy's cell phone rang, and as though she'd conjured her mom, Daisy's soft voice greeted her.

"How's my runaway middle child?"

"Oh, Mom. I haven't run away. Still in Pilgrim Cove. I moved into Sea View House today, and I'm a bit tired. You should know me better than to think I'd run back home because of a-a disappointment. My clock was ticking anyway."

"Great attitude. You're smart, talented, and those five-year-olds are darn lucky to have you in the classroom. I hope their parents realize that."

Her heart warmed as she thought of last year's group, all ready for first grade now. "I'm looking forward to another cool year. School starts a week from tomorrow, and I am so-o ready."

"Then you're really not coming back? Not even if Dad and I promise not to interfere with your life?"

Joy swallowed her laughter. If she allowed them, her family would suffocate her. "I love Pilgrim Cove. You should see the quarter moon hanging out right over my deck. The ocean's at my back door. Come and visit."

Daisy chuckled. "The same ocean puts me to sleep at night, honey. I see the same moon outside my window. Provincetown isn't that far away."

"True enough, but Mom? Don't worry about me. It'll all work out."

"We love you, Joy. Just the way you are. And someday, a wonderful man is going to gobble you up. Not everyone is a fertile Myrtle. And not everyone cares about it."

She'd give her mom an A for trying but ignored the message. If a man didn't care about kids, then he wouldn't be the right one for her. "I love you, too, Mom."

The porch door downstairs slammed, making Joy sit straighter. "Well, well, talk about returning home. My neighbor seems to have done just that after being gone all day. I think the lone wolf was afraid I'd ask him for help moving in."

"Some neighbor!"

"We'll see." She watched the yard below. Two shadows appeared, and she gulped. "Gotta go, Mom. Good night."

She disconnected, her eyes glued to the scene. How could she joke about a lone wolf when there was an actual one outside her home, gleaming silver in the moonlight? She rose from the lounge and gripped the railing, her heart thumping and her unblinking eyes moving slowly from man to beast.

CHAPTER THREE

"C'mon boy. Want to run?" Logan stepped toward the far wall of the yard. The dog moved to follow, then hesitated, sniffing the air. Logan looked left and right, then at the dark water. "Never saw the ocean before, is that it?"

Jax circled around him and faced the house, head back. He looked at Logan and emitted a small whine. Logan moved closer to the canine.

"Who's your friend, Mr. Nash?" A soft voice from the deck above.

He raised his eyes. In the moonlight, Joy MacKenzie's hair shone like a golden crown, and the cape she wore so proudly could have proclaimed royalty. Behind the soft tone and rigid stance, however, he detected something else. Something he'd seen and heard too many times in the past. Bravado.

"Nothing to be afraid of, Ms. MacKenzie. He's on our side. Come on down and meet Ajax." Might as well start the introductions now, as per the major's instructions.

"I'm not afraid of dogs, Mr. Nash. But he's big, and you haven't even leashed him."

"I was taking him for a run, but fair enough. I'll leash him. So, c'mon down."

She hesitated and looked away before responding. "I-I don't think so. Enjoy yourselves." She made for the door.

"You're going to have to meet him sooner or later."

She paused and faced him again. The blanket fell to the ground as she leaned forward on the railing. "Really? Why do I have to meet him? According to you, we're simply sharing a building…which barely qualifies us as neighbors."

A gotcha moment. He knew it. The girl was sharp. Had a brain and some stubbornness. "Point to you, Ms. MacKenzie. In our case, perhaps good fences don't make good neighbors, despite the opinion of Robert Frost."

Logan's lips moved, but his eyes locked on her. She not only had a mind but also a body. Her short-sleeved nightgown revealed skin as luminous as her light hair, and when the breeze blew…his breath caught. He'd been blind and stupid. She was no child. A woman stood on that balcony. Slender and petite. But all grown up.

"I totally agree," she said. "No fences for us. So, bring the wolf upstairs after your run. I'll make you a cup of tea."

"He's not a wolf."

"I know. But it's more fun to think he is."

His bubble burst. Fun? More like Fantasyland. So maybe she was still more child than adult. "I don't need tea. I'm not sick."

"For Pete's sake…I'm just trying to be neighborly, Mr. Nash."

He'd pick his battles. "Call me Logan."

"Yes! Finally." She fist-pumped the air and headed again to her door. "You are one stubborn man…oh, and I'm Joy."

The door slammed before he could argue, and he released a long breath. "Joy. Naturally. Well, it suits her, Ajax, but I sure don't know what to make of her. Maybe you'll figure it out. You've been perfect about everything else so far."

Any remaining doubts Logan had harbored about adopting Ajax had disappeared on the ride back. At their one rest stop, the dog had been perfect about heeling and bathroom activities. Logan had rewarded him with a biscuit and water. If his expression could be called "adoring," then Jax adored his old friend. Logan began to think that he and Jax were a team—with Logan as the alpha male. Just as it should be. He had Tommy to thank for that. The soldier had known how to establish the hierarchy of his tiny pack. And now all Logan had to do was follow suit.

He motioned to Ajax, and they both began to run along the beach. Maybe this Sea View House sojourn would work out after all.

"Careful where you step," Joy greeted a half hour later. "I moved in today." She opened the door wider and glanced around. "Guess I'm not quite settled in yet."

Logan glimpsed total chaos. Living in that mess would give him hives. She could take lessons from the military. He motioned to Ajax, and the dog sat perfectly on the threshold, his eyes on Logan.

"Ohh, he's even more beautiful up close." She glanced at Logan. "But you've got to admit, he's not your average-sized pooch."

"He's very well trained. C'mon, I'll introduce you. Just squat down and let him get to know you."

Her glance went from him to the canine and back again, remaining steady on him. "All right," she drawled, moving slowly to the dog and kneeling in front of him.

"This is Ajax." Then he repeated Joy's name several times while Ajax sniffed her hand. "Good boy," he said, giving him a treat. Jax sighed and lowered himself to a lying position.

"Tired baby," said Logan. "He's had a big day."

"I understand completely," Joy said with a laugh.

He made his way through the maze of cartons and boxes and sat at the kitchen table. A kettle whistled. He sensed Jax's alertness and motioned him to lie down again.

"He's amazing," said Joy.

"Yeah. You're not the first to say that."

She looked at him quizzically.

"Ex-military," he explained. "Retired."

Her eyes widened. "No wonder you keep saying he's well trained. I'm sure not going to worry about him anymore…not that I ever did." She turned around and began to pour the water into two mugs.

"Liar," he whispered. "But nothing to be ashamed of. Caution works best, especially around strangers—dogs or human."

She moved the mugs to within reach. "Is caution your general MO for living?"

He stiffened at her tone. A critique. But she immediately reached over and pressed his arm gently. "That was rude. I'm sorry."

His tension drained away. "You must get a lot of practice."

She cocked her head.

"Apologizing. It came quickly and naturally. So, do you usually speak before you think?"

Her forehead creased. She waited a beat. "I'm afraid the answer is yes." Her lips twitched, however, and her blue eyes gleamed as she said, "But you have to admit I gave a lot of thought to answering *that* question!"

He couldn't contain his own burst of laughter. She got high marks for honesty. Maybe she'd actually be a good housemate. The thought reinforced his earlier one. Sea View House might not be too bad.

##

"That sounds nice," said Joy. "Try laughing more often." All day long would be a good choice. The man was stunning with a generous smile framed by a scruffy beard. And those eyes! As warm and soft as a smoky gray mohair sweater.

Logan leaned back against the chair, scanning the place. "I moved in with one suitcase, a computer, printer, and my cameras. What's all this stuff?" He gestured around the room. "The house came furnished. How much can one person possibly need?"

Joy took a moment. "That's a loaded question." She saw his brow lift, eyes widen. The man didn't have a clue. "I suppose it depends," she said slowly.

"Go on."

"Is the place going to be a house or a home?" Heat rose to her cheeks. Somehow, they'd fallen into a very personal topic.

Leaning forward again, he said, "If there's a difference, I never noticed. House. Home. They're both the same to me."

Mere words couldn't do justice to an explanation. If the man hadn't experienced a real home, he wouldn't understand. Poor guy. He might even assume she was being dramatic. Her glance fell on Ajax.

"The dog needs a home, Logan, not just a house. Don't you see? He's part of your family now."

Smoke turned to steel. "Jax and I are a team. That's it. Just a team. We'll make out fine the way we are."

His protest gave her pause. "Of course you will," she affirmed. Somehow, she'd touched a raw spot with the word family, but it wasn't her business. Logan was an adult, not one of her precious little ones at school. Time to back off.

Her guest stood in one fluid motion. "Thanks for the tea." He looked around again. "And good luck with the…the conversion of the Crow's Nest. By the time you set it all up, Quinn will have found another place for you to live. That's the way it works."

"What are you talking about? He's looking, but it could—"

"Nope." He shook his head. "Just when you're getting comfortable… whack! Another house." His smile held traces of pity. "In the end, there's a lot to be said for a rolling stone." He headed for the door. "C'mon, Jax."

"Just a sec." Joy walked to the dog but addressed Logan. "Maybe he should meet Happy now, so he'll know everyone who lives here."

Logan rolled his eyes. "Sure. Just be glad Ajax isn't a hound dog."

Joy led them to the bird cage and whistled a series of clear notes. The bird returned the tune and sidestepped toward the door. "Hi, Happy. Want to meet our neighbors?" She opened the door slowly and offered her index finger. "Jax is trained to stay still, right?" she asked over her shoulder.

"Let's hope so," said Logan, motioning the stay order.

"Not funny," she mumbled, bringing Happy into the room. Jax turned his head, following every movement. Joy spoke to the dog while stroking the parakeet and continued the monologue when Happy spread his wings and took off around the room.

"Stay, Jax. He lives here." Logan's voice.

"He's like your brother," said Joy, glancing at the dog. "Understand?"

The canine's tail swished back and forth on the floor. His gaze followed the parakeet's flight until the bird returned to his cage.

After closing the door, Joy went to the dog and let him sniff her hand. "Happy belongs here with us," she said. She glanced at Logan but whispered to Ajax. "Just one big happy family at Sea View House."

##

The popular Diner on the Dunes, just east of Main Street on Dunes Boulevard, overflowed with the brunch crowd on Sunday. If Logan hadn't been so hungry, he would have forgone the meal and taken himself to the supermarket to stock up. A long walk with Jax at sunrise, however, seemed to have worked up Logan's appetite, and now his growling belly demanded attention.

The diner was a nautically themed white clapboard place. Round porthole-style windows marched across the walls near the roofline. All neat and tidy. He walked closer and halted in order to read a large red-and-white wooden sign over the door. *Home of the ROMEOs.* Logan grinned, shook his head, and pulled the knob. Bart Quinn had a way of making his presence felt. Logan stepped inside, and the coffee aroma hit his senses with a powerful thrust. He was salivating before he could greet the approaching server.

"Anywhere is fine," he said.

"Oh, no," said the young waitress, shaking her head. "Mr. Quinn said you're to follow me to his table. The big round one in the back."

Logan had wanted to get lost in the crowd, enjoy a quiet breakfast, and take in the atmosphere. He'd wanted to observe and absorb Pilgrim Cove on his own terms, at his own pace. He planned to attend the heavily advertised sand sculpture contest on the beach the next day, Labor Day. Just walk around, take some pictures. By himself. He wasn't a social butterfly like Bart Quinn or his upstairs neighbor. Quinn and Joy MacKenzie weren't related but were somehow cut from the same cloth. He sighed and followed the waitress.

"Sit down, sit down and join the party," boomed Quinn. "Have you met Sam Parker yet? He and his son run the plumbing and hardware store. And this is Doc Rosen, who somehow can't fully retire despite what his wife says."

Logan nodded to them, recognizing a few who'd been at Sea View House the day he'd moved in. The electrician, Ralph Bigelow. And Police Chief Rick O'Brien.

"Morning, folks." He pulled out a chair and joined the circle. "So this is the ROMEOs' hideout, huh?"

Bart Quinn smiled. "We have a few special places, but you can find some of us here for breakfast every day. And then there's The Lobster Pot. My daughters own it, the best restaurant in a hundred miles!" Pride shone on his face.

Logan reached for the cup of coffee in front of him, gave his breakfast order, and sat back. He'd been surrounded by a company of young men on the battlefront; now he was surrounded by a group of old men on the home front. He studied them one by one around the table, listening to their banter and the subtleties beneath. The only difference between the military men and the ROMEOs was age. The tightness and loyalty in each group were mirror images. As were their goals. Both groups were engaged in protecting their territories. Interesting. He wondered if these men were veterans. If there was a connection. If there was enough meat for a story.

"Has the magic gotten to you yet?" asked Bart.

Logan jerked from his reverie. "Magic? What are you talking about?"

"Have you not been listening? Sea View House. There's magic there if you let it in."

The guy wasn't daft. Just maybe…a romantic. A storyteller. Or a faithful kisser of the Blarney Stone. "Is there an old sea legend belonging to the house? Is that what you mean?"

"Of course there is, boy, but you'll have to ask Rachel and Jack Levine about that. They found each other and fell in love at Sea View House, but not without stormy times. The legend, too. Now it could be your turn."

Logan put up his hand. "I don't believe in magic, Mr. Quinn. So, I won't be having a turn."

Quinn's eyes almost popped from his head. "With that pretty little lass living above ya? You won't give it a chance?"

And have hives for the rest of his life? "That 'pretty little lass' is a…a wee bit unhinged, shall we say? A parakeet that she treats as a person? And a mess of stuff that overflows the entire apartment leaving no path to walk. She's totally disorganized…whenever I see her, she's running here, there, and everywhere. And to think she's in charge of a bunch of little kids! Save your breath, Mr. Quinn. And save your 'magic.'"

Bart looked at his contemporaries in disbelief. "The boy is blind. That little gal's just the ticket—cute as a button, smart, and kind. Everyone loves her. Why if I were twenty years younger…"

"Twenty?" laughed Doc Rosen.

"Okay, forty. Why, I'd be courting that girl as quickly as…as"—he snapped his fingers—"Fielding's greyhound runs the beach. That's how quick I'd be at her door."

A few laughs followed until Sam Parker raised his voice. "That's exactly what you did with Rosemary." Parker caught Logan's glance. "He met, courted, and married her in no time flat. And they stayed married for over forty years. Good years." He sighed. "We all miss her."

So Bart Quinn was a widower. Maybe a lonely one. "Not all men are like most of you seem to be," said Logan. He addressed Bart. "I'm glad you found your Rosemary, but I'm not the marrying kind. Right now, I'm between assignments, and my work takes me all over the world." He stared hard at the man. "I like it that way."

He spoke the truth about his lifestyle, and he'd have to figure out how to accommodate Ajax, but the old man wasn't totally off base about Joy MacKenzie. She was more than pretty. And the other night, when she'd stood on the deck in her nightgown with the breeze blowing against her, Logan's pulse had picked up speed. Briefly. Just for the moment. He was pretty sure he'd have reacted the same way with any woman. It had been a long time between dates. His next date, however, would definitely not be with the free-spirited Ms. MacKenzie, no matter how tempting she might be.

CHAPTER FOUR

She'd unpacked by the weekend. Hanging clothes in a closet was no problem, but organizing stuff took time. Needlework materials—knitting, crocheting, quilting— in two bins on her bedroom floor. Amazing how many leftover balls of yarn she had. Her paints, supplies, and easel would go into the second bedroom, her new studio.

According to her dad, everything needed a place or nothing would get done. "Let your imagination run wild," he'd say, "but not your work area." So she tried. And tried again. After starting out neat, she'd simply close her door when the inevitable happened. The same would occur here. Oh, well…

She hadn't seen much of Logan since the day she'd moved in. He usually took his camera and dog and disappeared for hours at a stretch. However, they had shared a second cup of tea the night before. While she'd chatted away, he hadn't shared anything personal. She wouldn't call them friends. At least, not yet.

Early on Labor Day morning, Joy dressed in shorts and a royal blue T-shirt and rubbed herself down with sunscreen. She gathered a variety of sand tools in a tote bag, grabbed her five-gallon painter's bucket, and made her way downstairs to the backyard of Sea View House. It was the most direct way to the beach. She hadn't counted on running into Logan or Ajax, but there they were, a handsome pair.

"Jax, you're beautiful. But you still look like a wolf to me." And darn if the dog didn't smile. She looked at Logan. "With that expression, how could anyone be afraid of him?"

Logan's mellow chuckle caught her by surprise. A wonderful sound. Almost musical. "What a difference a few days make, huh?"

She felt her cheeks get warm, probably turning a deep pink. "I really wasn't afraid," she protested, avoiding his gaze. "But if you're planning on taking Jax to the beach today, you can't. No dogs allowed in the summer until after Labor Day. And today, there's a bigger crowd than usual."

"The sand sculpting contest?"

She nodded.

He glanced at her paraphernalia. "You're entering?"

"It's my third time. I finally got the hang of it…I think. It's a lot of fun. Anyone can enter. Why don't you try it?"

"Nah…not my thing. I'll take a few pictures instead. Have a good time."

"I always do." She glanced at her watch. "Need to leave in order to get a good spot. Lots of folks sculpt, and the crowds have grown every year. See you later."

"I suppose you will."

Her eyes narrowed. "Cheer up. I'm not that bad." She jumped the stone fence at the end of the yard, separating the house from the beach, and headed toward the shoreline.

##

34

Joy eyed the beach the way a prospector eyed potential gold in the Yukon. Good sand. Bad sand. Good site. Bad site. Dross or gold. She looked for a spot a bit higher than the recent tide line but not too high or she'd be exhausted lugging buckets of water to the work area. She tested the sand an inch deep in a few areas. Did it hold together in a small ball when she rolled it between her palms? A lot to consider, but in almost no time, she found the perfect place and took up residence in her ten-by-ten allotted square.

She lugged a full pail of water and used it to pack down the sand. A strong base was mandatory. Twice more, she filled the bucket and carried it to her site. Good preparation. She would have gotten started on the actual piece sooner, however, if not for a steady stream of "Good morning, Joy." She waved at her friend who taught first grade, and then at two moms with kids who would be in her class that year. The little group paused.

"We're gonna build a sand castle," said the girl, a dimple peeking out when she grinned.

"As high as the sky," said the boy. He lifted his arms in emphasis, then frowned. "Or close."

"As high as you can, then," said Joy. "Good for you. Put lots of water on your sand so it will stick together."

They nodded in unison. Two cutie pies. Precious. Her heart turned over. She glanced at the moms. *Lucky ladies.* "Have a wonderful day with them."

"Not just a day, Ms. MacKenzie, but a wonderful year with you as their teacher. We'd hoped you'd stay in Pilgrim Cove," said the girl's mother.

"Being single and all," said her friend. "Pilgrim Cove is so small. I grew up here and left as soon as I could."

"But back you came," said Joy with a laugh.

The woman leaned closer. "Roots are hard to kill," she whispered. They waved and continued down the beach.

"Maybe…if you have them," murmured Joy. She took a knife from her tote bag, flipped the bucket upside down, and cut the bottom all the way around. She got rid of the bottom piece. She positioned the bucket firmly in the sand while Logan's image filled her mind. Rolling stones had no roots at all. They didn't seem to want any.

She poured four inches of sand into the bucket, added water to cover, and packed the sand down. Slowly. Carefully. Another four inches of sand. Another cover of water. Pack down. Sand, water, pack until she was about two inches from the top of the bucket.

She paused to gulp some fresh water from her thermos. More than an hour had passed since she'd arrived at the beach. She had almost two hours left to create her sculpture. Castle? Person? Storybook character? She hadn't even chosen a project, but she wasn't worried. Her hands would know. Her instincts would take over. That's how art often happened for her. *Trust the process*. Her mom's words.

Now came the test. With both hands, she smacked the sides of the bucket all the way around, then lifted it straight up. Yes! Tightly packed and ready to be carved.

She gathered her simple tools close—plastic fork, straws, spatula, spoon—and placed her hands lightly on the compacted sand. Her fingers began to play like a pianist warming up on the keyboard.

##

Logan began his stroll on the beach about an hour after Joy had left him in the backyard. First, he'd taken Jax on a long walk as was becoming their morning ritual. He wanted to instill a habit, get Jax comfortable with his new home and new routines. No problems in that department. In fact, adjusting to each other had been easy so far. He'd scheduled an appointment with the local vet, Adam Fielding, for later that week. Ajax needed a professional in his corner. And Logan needed a dog-loving confidant. The thoughts swirled as he continued to the shore.

Joy had called it. The place was packed. Colorful. With an excited vibe. An organizer's table had been set up. Logan took a flier listing the sand sculpting guidelines: Open to all ages; sculpting begins at nine and ends at noon; prizes awarded at one. He glanced at the rest of the list, pausing only to note the last rule: title your sculpture. Categories were divided by age. He pictured Joy, playing in the sand, as enthusiastic as any child, and laughed. "Adult" was surely the wrong category for her today! He wondered how she was making out but quickly became distracted by the efforts of other contestants.

He reached for his camera, checked the sun's position and his distance from the projects. He started taking candid shots, not disturbing anyone unless they chatted with him.

After thirty minutes, he mentally divided the beach between serious builders and fun-seeking families with kids whose sand castles collapsed almost as quickly as they rose.

"Better luck next time," he said after taking a quick shot of an adorable but disappointed face. The mom looked at him.

"Can I pay you for the picture? I know you're the pro at Sea View House, right? All my own pictures come out awful."

He hadn't come to Pilgrim Cove with the idea of earning money. He'd simply wanted to pull himself together. "No payment necessary." But the delivery? "Hmm…you know the Diner on the Dunes?"

"Of course," she replied with a laugh. "This is Pilgrim Cove. Everyone knows everything."

Yup. She was right. "I'll leave the photo with the hostess. Check for it by the end of the week." Easier to leave a print than start exchanging email addresses.

He meandered, absorbed the scene. An aqua-tinted ocean, waves lapping the shore. A colorful array of folks enjoying their last day of summer. There'd be a parade later on that evening. And it reminded him that the freedom to celebrate America was what Tommy had died defending, whether Labor Day or any other holiday. He wondered if anyone on the beach gave a thought to the soldiers. Or if they cared.

His gaze wandered and stopped short. He couldn't miss that royal blue shirt and the floppy hat. In the near distance, Joy MacKenzie moved in a circle dance. He couldn't see her piece but knew she was concentrating full force on it. Like a magpie, she flew high and low, then paused and cocked her head, thinking. He walked toward her, his camera ready. Didn't wonder about the reason. Didn't care about what she'd sculpted. He'd use a high shutter speed to freeze the action.

Fully focused on his goal, he didn't speak, didn't call attention to himself, didn't let his gaze wander to anything but Joy. *Click. Click.* Fluttering up and down. *Click, click.* Studying her work, hands on hips, a frown on her forehead. *Click, click.* Eyes shining in resolve. He watched—and clicked—as she stooped low and blew gently through a straw, removing excess sand from her statue.

With his peripheral vision, he noted a small crowd had gathered to observe. A quiet group. Unbelievably, the social butterfly ignored them. Interesting. Joy was obviously more than an amateur in the sand sculpting business.

"What time is it?" she asked no one in particular.

"Quarter of."

Logan checked his watch and nodded. She had fifteen minutes before the contest ended. He stepped closer, now curious about her subject. Castle? Dragon? Princess? Nothing could have prepared him for the reality.

Ajax. A perfect doppelganger. On his haunches. Beautiful. But she'd carved that stupid smile on him with his tongue hanging out. And…he squinted…what was that thing sitting on his head? He moved closer. For Pete's sake! A stupid parakeet. His body tensed; his heart pounded.

She glanced over and a smile grew. "You found us!"

"What have you done?" he roared. "He looks like a fool."

Shocked at himself, he not only heard but also felt the silence that followed his outburst. Maybe he'd leave this town. Too many people in each other's business. He belonged on the sidelines. The periphery had always been his comfort zone. He never got involved, never shouted. Never cared about anyone or anything, for that matter. Except for Tommy and Jax, his first real family. And look how that wound up.

To Joy's credit, she tempered her surprise with a mere slight angling of her head. "Folks," she said, "this dog is for real. His name is Ajax and he's certainly no fool. He's the most wonderful dog you can imagine. The fool in this conversation is standing right next to me. His name is Logan Nash, and he's new in town. Needs a lot of TLC after spending a couple of years in Iraq."

He sensed the crowd's suspicion changing to sympathy. Except for Joy. Her glare carried a message even he could read. *You're a stupid ass.*

"I think you'll feel better when you see the title I'm using," she said. Without waiting for an answer, she sprinkled water on the sand near Jax's front paws. Quick, quick, quick, she shaped four capital letters. "HERO."

"I was going to call it 'Bird Dog' because *Ajax has a sense of humor*. But I wanted to honor him, too. So 'Hero' it is."

The back of his neck tingled. He felt the flush on his face. Way to go, Nash. Creating a public scene with the darling of the town. There was only one thing to do: surrender.

"You've done a beautiful job, Ms. MacKenzie." He scanned the crowd. "Sorry to disturb the party. If you ever want to meet Ajax—the real flesh-and-blood one—just knock on my door."

The words came awkwardly. He had no practice issuing invitations. "For the record, Jax has led over four hundred missions, and no one was ever hurt by an IED when following him."

Questions flew, and Logan found himself surrounded by curious people who wanted to shake his hand. People who invited him and Jax for dinner. His skin itched. "I'm no hero!" he said. "I'm just a guy with a camera. Never carried a rifle. Just a camera, computer, and a pen."

"A pen can slice sharper than a knife, young man."

He pivoted to see an older woman in dark glasses, salt-and-pepper hair pulled back, and holding a little girl's hand. "Only an English teacher would say something like that," he replied.

The lady laughed with a sound of delight and held her arm out in his general direction. He stepped closer and took her hand. "I'm Logan Nash."

"I'm Marie Oakley, and guilty as charged. Used to teach English in the Boston high schools. And this little one is my granddaughter, Bonnie."

"Hi, Bonnie."

The child peeked out from behind her grandma and didn't say a word.

"I don't blame you," said Logan. "Too many people, huh?"

The girl nodded and pointed at Joy. "She's my teacher." Soft words carried by a gentle breeze.

"Well, aren't you the lucky one." Not. Joy wasn't a good match for this shy child. She'd probably force her into the middle of a dozen group activities on the first day of school.

"We certainly are lucky," said Marie. "Bonnie needs a nice young woman in her life. Joy MacKenzie is perfect for her."

"Maybe…but what's really perfect is the way you two nestle into each other. Good composition." He reached for his Nikon. "Mind if I take a shot?"

"Please do. It'll be a memory for Bonnie. A good memory."

He stilled. An underlying sadness echoed in her voice, and yet, they were both here. Healthy, to his eye. "It will be a memory for both of you."

Marie smiled and remained quiet.

Click. Click. He walked a few steps. "Don't feel like smiling, pretty Bonnie?"

She shook her head.

"Want to give Grandma a kiss?"

She tilted her head back and lifted to her toes. *Click. Click*. Marie leaned closer to the child. *Click, click*.

"I love you, Grandma."

He caught Marie's flash of despair with his camera, the shine of incipient tears.

"And I love you, too, sweetheart." She kissed the little one's cheek. Bonnie's arms wrapped around her.

His journalist's instincts rose to high alert. There was a story here that made him uneasy. If he remained at Sea View House long enough, however, he'd uncover it.

CHAPTER FIVE

Standing on her deck each evening had become a routine for Joy. She never tired of the view. Or of the ocean's white noise, a lullaby that calmed and kept her company. On the evening after Labor Day, another sight greeted her. Logan and Ajax. Two handsome and vigorous males, jogging along the shoreline on the hard-packed sand. Because of high tide, they weren't too far away, and she was able to track them.

Logan must have remembered that dogs were allowed on the beach now. He obviously wanted to provide Jax the freedom to run. If she ever adopted a dog, she'd let him run, too. Pets, however, were not on her immediate agenda. The start of the school year was. And tomorrow was the first day.

Her neighbors disappeared from view, and loneliness wrapped itself around her. Sighing, she admitted that her emotions were tricky to control these days. Tears came when she least expected them. She pounded the top of the railing. Acceptance! She had to accept that her ovaries were gone. Her new regimen included hormone replacement through pills. Since her surgery a month ago, she'd faithfully swallowed them, one each night. And each time, she didn't know whether to punch the wall or cry. The moment would pass, however, and she'd go about her daily life, keeping the miserable fact to herself.

Everyone thought she was a happy-go-lucky person with not a care in the world. Maybe once upon a time, she had been. Not anymore.

The breeze picked up, and she shivered in her crocheted sweater. If she'd gone running with the "boys," she'd be toasty warm. But she hadn't been invited, and after yesterday's flare-up with the sand sculpture, she figured Logan had had enough of Pilgrim Cove and certainly enough of her. After all, she'd called him a fool with no sense of humor.

"Hey, Joy! Joy MacKenzie."

She twirled in the direction of the voice. Logan ran toward the house, elbows bent, his legs moving like pistons. The dog kept up the pace, sticking to his man's side as though they were yoked together.

The pair slowed down when they reached the backyard, and Joy waited while Logan gulped air and caught his breath, waited to hear what he had to say.

He tipped his head back and smiled. "How'd you make out in the contest yesterday?"

The warmth of that smile made her breath hitch and fogged her brain. "What?"

"'Hero.' How did we make out?"

"We?" she asked in astonishment. "We? Let's say that Jax and took second place." Logan had disappeared right after taking pictures of Marie and Bonnie.

"Only second? But you did a great job. I walked that beach, and nothing else compared." He stepped closer. "Are you disappointed?"

His gentle tone confused her. The Logan Nash she knew wouldn't be concerned about her feelings. Maybe she was growing on him.

"Of course not. I had a wonderful time building the piece. It was fun. And let's face it, sculpting sand is sort of…shall we say…a disappearing art?" She grinned, waving her fingers toward the sea.

He threw back his head and emitted a deep laugh. Warm and rich. Musical. She could have listened for hours. "Want a cup of tea…or hot chocolate?"

His gaze lingered on her for a moment. "Give me five minutes to shower."

##

She was only being neighborly. That's what Joy told herself as she boiled water and arranged mugs. But maybe that was what Logan needed. He was new in town. Didn't know many folks. She could help him… Yeah. Right. The guy needed as much help as…as the man in the moon. It was she who needed her head examined.

A staccato rap on her door interrupted her thoughts. Happy flew to her shoulder as she let the man in. She peered around him. "Where's Ajax?"

"Hunkered down on his bed. Maybe the run was too much. I keep forgetting he's ten years old."

"I think he forgets, too! It's a good way to be." She led him inside the kitchen and stepped toward the stove.

"I'm not sure," said Logan. "I'm not into pretending. I like dealing with reality."

Reality sucked. Hers anyway. She tilted her head and looked up at him. "Sometimes it's a state of mind. If Jax feels younger, he'll act younger and be happier."

"I think he's happy living with me—so far. He's got an appointment with the vet tomorrow." His voice

45

quieted, and he stared over her shoulder, avoiding her eyes.

She moved the hot milk from the burner and stepped away from the stove. Instinctively, she squeezed his arm. "Jax is fine."

Under her fingers, she felt his muscles flex, then still. The man himself remained still. Said nothing. She sensed his unease and lifted her hand. She heard him inhale before facing her.

"Ajax is fine now," he said. "But…nothing lasts. Just like all those castles in the sand yesterday, one day he'll disappear, too. Everyone does. They come and go. I don't know why, but that's the way it works. You're old enough to understand that."

Now Joy had to take a breath. A deep one. She stood as tall as she could. "For the record, I'll be thirty on my next birthday. I understand a lot." She paused, let it sink in. "I've earned two college degrees, hold a responsible job, and am old enough to know that you're wrong."

He backed away from her, his gray eyes dark thunderclouds. "I wish I were wrong! But I'm not. If you think people hang around forever, then you've spent almost thirty years living under a rock. Or maybe hanging out too long in Pilgrim Cove."

She may have garnered two degrees, but she wasn't a psychologist. Neither fact, however, prevented her from plunging ahead. "My parents have been married for thirty-eight years. I have a younger sister and older brother. We're all in touch and happy with each other. Is that enough to convince you that most people don't just up and leave?"

Silence. It could have been a gotcha moment, but that hadn't been her goal. His ideas about life were polar opposite to hers and tore a corner of her heart. She walked closer, put her palms against his cheeks. "I'm sorry, Logan. Sorry for your pain."

He jerked back. "Don't waste your pity, sweetheart. Your folks are the exception to the rule. Just look at us, for example."

"Us? We're strangers…"

"And always will be. This place is a way station. No matter how Bart Quinn presents it, Sea View House is just a shelter for people with no other place to go."

"Not true! You've got a condo in Boston, and Bart's looking for a new apartment for me." She reached for his arm again. She'd always been a toucher, no question about it. A toucher and a hugger. But Logan wanted no part of connecting. She had to rely on words.

"There's a good bit of magic in this 'way station,' Logan Nash. Ask anyone. In fact, ask the vet you're going to visit tomorrow. It's not hocus-pocus magic, just a gentle magic that touches the heart. And that's all I'm going to say—for now. My lips are sealed." She pressed them together for emphasis.

No way was she going to tell Logan about the marriages that had occurred for prior residents of Sea View House. She could think of three or four immediately.

His eyes narrowed, then gleamed. She'd gotten his attention. "How can one little girl be so stubborn?"

"Easy."

His brow lifted.

"Because I'm right. And…I'm not a little girl." She stuck her chin out. Might as well go for the jugular. "You seem to prefer viewing me as jailbait, and I can't help wondering why."

He hesitated a moment, perhaps to argue the point. Instead, he slowly nodded at her. "Because it's safer that way. Easier, too."

"Just what I thought," she said. "You're a coward. Friendships are too messy for you."

His nostrils flared. His mouth tightened. She sensed his control, his rigid control as he studied her from head to foot. It didn't deter her from continuing.

"You think relationships aren't worth your effort. After all, they might not work out."

"You have no idea what you're talking about."

She shrugged. "We're social animals, Logan. People need each other. Your false barriers won't work."

Logan headed for the door. "Thanks for the hot chocolate, Jailbait. It was very neighborly of you."

She watched him leave, an echo of her own words remaining in her head. People needed people, just as the song advised. At least she had her family, job, and a slew of friends in Pilgrim Cove and elsewhere. She did relationships pretty well. She'd focus on the ones she had and learn to live without the one she'd have treasured most of all.

No falling in love allowed.

##

If she'd goaded him a little more, he would have run another few miles on the beach by himself. False barriers? The girl knew squat and didn't know when to shut up. Like picking a scab or rubbing salt on a wound, she kept on talking. A woman like her wouldn't know about loneliness. Or about being alone year after year. With that all-American family she bragged about, she wouldn't understand any of it.

They'd all let him down. Mother. Father. Grandma. One by one, they'd all left him. He'd been a young kid, so what was he to think? He blamed himself. His fault. Thank God, he'd eventually discovered art in high school. And then photography. Although his talents hadn't won him any friends, his teachers had encouraged him. Drawing kept him going through every disappointment.

Nah, Joy MacKenzie wouldn't understand abandonment if it bit her on the arm. Best to keep away from her.

Logan couldn't judge whether the vet's office was typical or not. A large yellow tabby roamed a high catwalk and, with her aloof expression, looked as if she owned the place. A beautiful greyhound dog lay next to the front desk, ignoring the receptionist, probably thinking it owned the place, too. And a young girl with curly dark hair and a backpack over her shoulders dashed toward the door, calling her good-byes. She halted abruptly, however, when she saw Jax in the waiting room.

"Oh, you beauty," she exhaled, walking right over to the shepherd and talking softly to him. Looking up at Logan, she said, "I hope I get to know him when I have more time. But I can't miss the bus on the first day of school."

Joy's image popped into his mind. He'd heard her clatter down the stairs over an hour ago. "Sure," he replied to the little one in front of him. "Visit whenever you want. Jax and I are at Sea View House."

"Really?" she squealed. "My new mom lived there, too. And then she met my dad and now...now..." She twirled around, arms wide, backpack and all. Logan reached to catch her if she tipped. "And now we're all married," she continued. "We're all together, and I'm so happy."

Was it a conspiracy? A Sea View House conspiracy? Or was he in a scene from Alice in

Wonderland? "Have a great day," he muttered as she finally ran out the door. So it was the kid who actually owned the place…with her folks.

"She used to be shy."

Logan turned and clasped the vet's outstretched hand. The man wore dark scrubs and a twinkle in his green eyes. "Adam Fielding," he said. "Glad to finally meet you, Mr. Nash." He immediately leaned down toward the shepherd. "Hello, Ajax." He offered his fist for the dog to sniff. "I'm delighted to meet you, too. Want to go for a walk?"

Jax's ears twitched, but he looked toward Logan.

"Perfect. Exactly what I like to see. Now take him for a stroll around the room. We'll check out his gait."

Half an hour later, Logan knew he'd found a professional to rely on. "I have to admit, you're making me feel a hell of a lot more confident. Jax and I have been through some tough times, but he was never mine. And now, I'm all he's got."

"He couldn't have done better." Fielding's gaze swept toward the greyhound on the floor. "Ginger is a rescue that my daughter wouldn't part with. I've been finding homes for retired greyhounds for years, and now, with my practical wife, we're starting to find homes for all breeds or no breed at all. So when I say that Jax is in the perfect home with the perfect owner, I know what I'm talking about."

Logan swallowed hard at the unexpected praise. He was used to compliments about his work but not about his personal qualities. He was far from perfect. As a human being, he sucked. He knew it. He pushed people away and didn't care. That had always been his MO, and it worked. His life worked.

He glanced from the veterinarian to Ajax and blinked fast. He now recognized the lie he told himself. Joy had recognized it, too, and had called him on it.

Accused him of erecting "false barriers." She was right, but the barriers had protected him. Now they'd be around both him and Jax.

"Thanks. Thanks very much for your vote of confidence. I…I needed to hear that."

"It's the truth. So, on a personal note—I've followed all your stories. I'm a fan and proud to know you."

He wasn't expecting another compliment and just nodded.

"How about coming for dinner?" Fielding asked. "Rebecca would be happy to meet you. You've got something in common. She never owned a dog either until she lived in Sea View House—and met me, of course."

The man's face turned ruddy. "What the hell?" he asked with a laugh. "We just returned from a short honeymoon, but I swear, it keeps going."

Listening to the vet talk was like watching a character in a play. That kind of happiness didn't last. The man was heading for a fall and had no clue. But it would happen. Act II always happened. And who would clean the mess up in Act III? Nope. Not getting involved.

"Thanks, Doc. I'll let you know. I'm just settling in."

"Call me Adam. I remember being the new guy in town here. Just little Sara and me, looking for a new start. Bart Quinn found this place for us…and was welcoming, but…I could have used a buddy my own age."

Logan felt himself relax again. "We think alike there. The man's great, but enough is enough."

He paid the bill and, with Jax on his leash, left the office whistling a cheerful tune—which reminded him of the magpie and the budgie. Shaking his head, he reached for the camera strapped to his waist. The sand sculpture contest had been a surprise. He'd been out and about since arriving in Pilgrim Cove ten days earlier, exploring the possibilities in a small beach town. People in their environment. Candid photos revealing the substance of lives, the ordinary and the extraordinary. And the surprises. That was what he liked best. With his camera, he could reveal the essence of his subjects.

He headed toward the diner to drop off yesterday's beach pictures as promised. The shots had turned out well, and the parents would be happy. That grandma, too. For a moment, he felt a frisson of concern as he remembered Marie with her little Bonnie. He shook it off, however, and his heart became as light as his step. He was a good dad for Jax, and that's all that mattered.

The sun cast long shadows as Joy raced down the driveway toward her door. Her tote bag swung on her arm, hitting her thigh as she ran. The first day of school had sped by in a blink, and now a host of ideas and images flashed through her mind, ideas for the eighteen children in her class. Eighteen individual children at various skill levels and with different developmental needs. Some knew the alphabet letters, others didn't. Some knew numbers, others did not. Some were confident, while others hung back. That last item, confidence, was key to the others, and more important, key to a happier life. She faced lots of prep work for her class, and she itched to get started.

Click. Wrrr. She turned at the sound and spotted Logan striding from the backyard, camera in hand. Before she could say a word, however, Jax bounded toward her. The shepherd looked at Logan once but never paused in his route. Reaching Joy, he whined and sat in front of her, nose up and tail wagging against the ground. She couldn't resist. She dropped her bag and snuggled him, scratching behind his ears.

"You good boy. Handsome boy. I missed you, too. Did you have a great day?"

The canine drowned her in kisses, and she leaned back, laughing. "What a homecoming, Ajax! But I can't play now. I have work to do." Straightening, she saw her neighbor had closed the distance between them. "Hello, Logan. And...Mr. Nikon. Are you working on another project?"

His flash of surprise was quickly followed by a self-deprecating grin. "I wouldn't use the term work. You know how we creative folk are. Everyone says we just follow our muse and play."

She chuckled but shook her head. "Puh-leeze! That's a lot of baloney. I know how creative folk are. I come from a family of them. And they all make sure their 'muse' is in gear every single day so they'll be paid when the work is finished. Artists have to eat, too."

He leaned forward. All traces of sarcasm disappeared. "So that explains it."

"Explains what?" she asked, wondering if she'd missed a clue.

"You."

"Me?" She cocked her head, felt her brow crease.

"Yeah. You've been on my mind a lot, but I can't...exactly figure you out. You dress weird and act like such a...a...ditz. But then you come through. You confuse me," he finally said.

The insult to her colorful style and many vintage choices wasn't as important as his revelation. "Good. It's time someone did." The man had great potential as a human being. He simply needed shaking up—and she'd be happy to do it. For his own good, of course.

He grimaced and pulled at his ear lobe. "Tell me more," he said quietly, "about your family. You said they were all creative?" His words caught her off guard, but his manner caught her attention. He seemed unusually interested. Ordinarily she would have probed for more information and chatted, but she saw an opportunity to rattle him.

She grabbed her tote and opened the door. "Sorry. Don't have time. Besides, you've made it perfectly clear that we're merely neighbors and cannot be friends." With an unblinking stare, she said with slow deliberation, "My life…is private to casual acquaintances."

She let the door slam behind her and ran upstairs, proud of her smashing exit. Her sister would have been proud, too. Glory's career in the theater had been growing, and now she was in a revival of *Who's Afraid of Virginia Woolf?* opening in Boston very soon. The slammed door, however, wasn't about Glory. It was all about Logan. She'd crack his shell if it took all winter.

With that thought, she wondered why she cared. Sure, she had a soft heart, but it was usually reserved for children. Logan was no child! When she pictured his gray eyes studying her, his scruffy beard and broad chest with the defined pecs, a warmth rushed through her body, starting from the center and traveling to fingers and toes. It made her breath catch.

Logan Nash turned her on.

It wouldn't be easy, but she'd simply have to ignore it. Her life was too complicated now and would never change.

But why had he asked about her family? Surely not from idle curiosity. There was a lot about the MacKenzies that Logan might find interesting. Too bad he acted like a jerk. Except when he didn't. Like with Ajax. With the kids on the beach. Offering free pictures to their moms. The women likely had no idea who'd captured their children in his lens.

In fact, she really didn't know his work, either. He was a puzzle that she hadn't yet solved, so he wasn't alone in his confusion. She powered up her computer and started searching. Her classroom prep work would have to wait.

An hour later, she wiped her eyes and filled the kettle. Anyone who produced a series like Soldiers of a Different Breed deserved a cup of hot chocolate at the end of the day. With no phone number for Logan, she ran downstairs, around to the back door, and rapped hard.

It swung open immediately. Man and dog stood on alert. "What's wrong? What happened?" Logan asked, pulling her inside while scanning the yard behind her. Ajax had begun sniffing the threshold and adjacent perimeter of the floor.

"N-nothing," she whispered. "Nothing happened. I didn't have your number, and I was making some chocolate…"

If looks could kill…

"Chocolate? You scared me to death over chocolate?"

"Scared you? Could it be you overreacted?"

He motioned to Jax and spoke simultaneously. "Stop." The dog's head came up and he waited. "Come," said Logan, again using both voice and hand signals. Jax trotted to Logan, who scratched his ruff. "Good boy."

Logan took a ball from his pocket. Held it out to the dog and tossed it across the room. Jax was on it in a flash and immediately brought it back.

The man glanced at Joy. "Play is the reward for work. When you knocked loudly on the door, he was on the job." He tossed the ball again.

"Oh. Sorry. I-I thought you wouldn't hear me if I just tapped."

His eyes gleamed. A smile crossed his face, and when he began to laugh with his musical sound, she shivered down to her toes and felt heat rise to her face. She wanted to disappear.

Logan met her gaze openly—no shadows, no furrows—six foot of handsome, and now a straight shooter with more than just a camera. He stepped closer and drew her farther into the room.

"We'd certainly know if you tapped on the door. At least, Jax would. His hearing is four times more acute than ours."

His words reminded her of the story she'd finished reading. "Of course," she said. "I wasn't thinking. But now I know how remarkable he and his pals are thanks to Soldiers of a Different Breed."

"Change the topic," he ordered, the lines across his brow reappearing.

Surprised at his curt tone, she studied him, saw the pain, and nodded. "All right," she said slowly. "But fair warning: if you keep writing stories and taking pictures that bring your subjects to life, I will become your biggest fan girl…and how would you handle that?"

From pain to heat, the reflection in his eyes changed in a second. Embers glowed as hot and steady as molten steel. So Mr. Logan Nash wasn't the hermit, wasn't as disinterested as he wanted to be. As he wanted folks to believe…as he'd like *her* to believe.

He drew her closer. "Like this," he muttered. "I'd handle you like this." His fingers lay lightly on her shoulders as he lowered his head. Her senses rocked with anticipation. She forgot about her worries, her life plan. All she saw was Logan.

When their lips touched, her heart raced and a delicious shudder ran through her body. Such a fast reaction, and different than with any man she'd kissed before Logan. She wasn't an ingénue…but this! This was exciting. A new facet of herself. Standing on her tiptoes, she wrapped her arms around his neck. She wanted more connection. More of him.

He showered kisses along her jaw, up to her earlobe. And finally, his mouth covered hers with a hunger she understood—and matched. When his lips parted, hers did also. When his tongue teased hers, she rode the wave, and her ordinary world disappeared in the mist.

Finally…somehow…they stepped away from each other. She could hear him breathing. She knew he could hear her gasps.

"My, oh, my," she whispered. "That was a…a surprise." More like a shock.

He cocked his head. "I thought with one kiss, I'd get you out of my system, but"—a tiny sideways grin appeared—"you're a surprise, all right. Maybe even a good one."

Her plan had totally failed. In trying to shake him up, she'd shaken herself. He was definitely human, more than a "project." Her meddling could cause them both more pain.

CHAPTER SIX

Joy tossed and turned thinking about the kiss. About Logan. He'd been a different man after that kiss, a carefree, relaxed, and happy Logan. A lighter heart looked good on him. And she kept her reservations to herself. So what if they got involved with each other temporarily? He wouldn't be in town for long. A bit of R and R and he'd be off on a new assignment, following a good story and focusing his lens to capture it. They were both adults. They'd accept change. They'd accept a good-bye. She squeezed her lids shut as she pictured the scene, as she pictured hope fading from Logan's eyes.

At least they'd exchanged phone numbers. Small comfort after the fact. She turned on her side for the umpteenth time, forced herself to lie still. And only then heard the waves lapping against the shore. Over and over in a steady rhythm, a lullaby to everyone along the coastline. Her breaths became synchronized with the tide, and slowly she drifted off.

When she walked into her classroom the next morning, her ordinary world came into focus. Her concerns about Logan diminished as she concentrated on the children. She greeted each one by name, directed them to their cubbies to deposit their backpacks, and then led them to the big red circle mat on the floor. Each day started with a "morning meeting" and a good-morning song. A nice way to settle in—and take attendance.

Only seventeen. She noted Bonnie's absence and bit her lip. Yesterday, the child had been a delight, following directions and closely observing her new environment. A kindergarten classroom. She'd certainly seemed happy enough. Joy wondered if she'd get a message about Bonnie later in the day. If not, she'd call Marie herself.

From the red mat, Joy directed her students to their table clusters. It was time to work with numbers, and today *three* would take center stage. She retrieved her box of pencils, books, Popsicle sticks, and a variety of other counting objects. Before she had time to begin, however, Bonnie appeared in the doorway, holding on to Sara Fielding's hand. Joy smiled at the girls.

"Hi, Sara. Hi, Bonnie. I'm so glad to see you."

"She was late," said Sara. "I'm the office monitor this morning, so I brought her to your class." She turned toward Bonnie. "Give Ms. McKenzie your late pass."

Bonnie stuck her hand out, the paper in it.

"Thank you, Bonnie. And thanks, Sara, for keeping her company. Good job!"

The fifth grader smiled and headed back down the corridor to the front office. Joy kneeled to Bonnie's eye level.

"I'm happy you came to school today," she said while finger combing the child's long windblown hair. "We would all miss you."

The girl nodded. "I love school," she whispered, her arms wide open. "But...I-I missed the bus."

Did her grandmother know? Had she walked to school all by herself? Joy tacked the questions to the back of her mind. Later. She'd think about them later. Now, she had eighteen children to care for.

##

Two men stood on the front porch of Sea View House when Joy pulled into the driveway after work. One made her heart race, the other made her laugh. Logan Nash and Bart Quinn. Oy.

Logan waved her over as soon as she exited her car. As she got closer, she noticed the loose-leaf binder Quinn held. "Is that a real estate book? Did you find a new place for me?"

Before the older man could answer, Logan chimed in. "I bet not. Everything's on computer these days. Unless he has a laptop in that classic Lincoln Town Car of his, I wouldn't bet he's found anything." A definite note of satisfaction laced his voice.

"I don't need a computer," Bart replied, his voice booming. "That's my granddaughter's job. Lila's my partner, you know. She's got to earn her keep!" He chuckled and pointed at his forehead. "It's all in here. Every listing we've got in the whole county. As for the details…well, I've got a binder that holds everything. And it's a lot bigger than this one." He looked at the notebook in his hand.

"As long as we've got that settled, how about we all sit down?" asked Joy, motioning to the cushioned chairs on the porch. She glanced meaningfully at Logan, the downstairs resident.

"Absolutely," he said. "Or better yet, come on inside, out of the wind. The season's changing."

The Captain's Quarters looked like a military barracks, or at least how Joy perceived one to be. Neat as a pin. Everything in its place. Logan led them down the hall to the living room. Wide-planked oak floors extended throughout the house; a red brick fireplace in the colonial-style living room ran to the ceiling, definitely the main focal point.

"This place is scary," Joy said as she greeted the dog. "But you're not scary, are you, sweet boy?"

"Scary?" Logan's mouth fell open.

"It's too neat and clean. Is there room for a speck of dust anywhere?"

He gave her an incredulous stare. "And that's a crime? I almost choked in your place. What a mess."

Quinn looked from one to the other before lowering himself to the cushioned maple rocker near the couch. "Perfect," he said. "Absolutely perfect. The magic's already working."

"So what's going on, Mr. Quinn?" asked Joy, choosing a club chair opposite the older man. "What's perfect?"

"The possibilities, my girl. The possibilities." He waved the notebook in front of them. "Read the *Sea View House Journal*, and you'll understand everything."

Quinn glanced directly at Logan. "Your new friend, Adam Fielding, is in here. He and his Rebecca found each other when she lived right here in this very house. And that was only a few months ago! And last month they got married."

"I-I was away," Joy said quickly. "Missed it." Hospital images teased her. Lying in bed, long hallways, operating room lights, and her doctor squeezing her hand, speaking softly. *We've been through this before, and of course, we'll try to save the ovary one more time.*

But she'd seen the truth in his eyes. Her cysts were unrelenting despite all the treatments and therapies.

Quinn's voice brought her back. "You were having a grand old time in Provincetown, weren't you, Joyful?"

He glanced at Logan, leaned forward. "Her folks work their own kind of magic. Beauty that can make your heart cry or dance."

Joy suppressed a smile. The old guy had a way with words. Always had, but this time she agreed with each one of them.

"I never met them, but I looked them up recently," said Quinn. "So now I can say for sure. They do the work of angels."

True. Her dad was designing an outdoor sculpture for the Central Park Zoo in New York while also preparing for a gallery show of small pieces in Boston. Her mom's latest stained glass scene from the Old Testament had been commissioned by a church in Philadelphia. She combined that work with her Daisy Mac line of jewelry, which had hit a sweet spot with buyers. Not only beautiful but different and affordable.

"There's nothing like family to create great memories," said Quinn. "Or a camera to capture them." He nodded at Logan. "You could be one of that clan, my boy. Magic comes out of your camera."

One glance at Logan's expression and Joy had to control her laughter. The old man could have said poison and gotten the same reaction.

"I take good shots because I use my eyes. I don't invoke a bunch of hocus-pocus. I'm disappointed, Quinn. You're sprouting a lot of baloney."

Joy knew a lot more than "eyes" went into a brilliant composition. It took years of acquired skill and learning. If it were easy, anyone could do it.

Quinn raised his arm, the book in his hand. "After you read what's inside the Sea View House Journal, you'll change your mind. Anything can happen here, and these real-life stories prove it." He gave the journal to Logan, who immediately passed it to Joy.

"You first. I don't have time."

"School just started. Neither do I." She returned it.

He walked to the bookshelves lining the far wall and slipped it into an end space. "It'll be waiting for you there, Mr. Quinn. Safe and sound."

For one moment, the leader of the ROMEOs, the guy who gave the Blarney Stone a good name, seemed at a loss for words. "Stubborn!" he finally said. "That's what you are. I've never seen two more stubborn people."

"How about looking in the mirror?" asked Logan, a smile removing the sting from his words. "I've got a question for you, Bart Quinn. Have you ever lived in Sea View House yourself?"

The man startled, then seemed to recall a faraway memory as his eyes brightened. "Never had to," he said. "Met my Rosemary before Sea View House became what it is today. Such good years. She's been gone for ten. But she's still..." His voice choked as he tapped his chest.

Joy met Logan's intense gaze, nodded, and addressed Bart Quinn. "It seems to me," she began, "you could use a bit of that Sea View House magic yourself."

"The spirit you believe in so much," added Logan in a tone that challenged the other man to put his money where his mouth was.

"Me?" spluttered Quinn. "I've already had the magic. My Rosemary."

"Is a person limited to just once in a lifetime?" asked Joy. "You're a handsome, witty man, Mr. Quinn. Just look at that head of white hair—like a lion's mane. You've got a lot of life ahead of you. No reason you can't benefit from the Sea View House legend."

Quinn stood up fast, leaving the rocking chair close to overturning. "This house is not about me. It's for the young."

"You *are* young—" began Joy.

"She's right," interrupted Logan. "With all due respect, you and Ajax here are about the same age, and he's got a long way to go yet, according to Adam Fielding."

"Bah humbug," said Quinn. "I'm giving you kids good advice. Relax, open your hearts, and feel the magic. It's yours for the taking." He walked toward the door, calling over his shoulder, "I can see myself out. I hope I didn't make a mistake with you two."

Joy sat quietly for a moment after the man exited, then said to Logan, "Forget about us. But I like Mr. Quinn, and I think we shook him up. A lot. I'm having second thoughts. Maybe we came on too strong."

"Oh, we shook him up, all right, but save your concern. We've got him thinking. He had a question in his eye. A new idea. But the real tell…?" Logan leaned over her. "He lost his cool. Protested too much."

"I hope you're right…"

The front door opened and the man in question reappeared. "With all your nonsense, I almost forgot the second reason I came here." He pointed a finger at Logan, then at Joy. "You're both invited for dinner at The Lobster Pot this Friday night. And it's on the house. My daughters want to meet and feed my new tenants."

"But…" began Joy. After two years in town, she'd already met Thea Cavelli and Maggie Sullivan and, more importantly, devoured their food.

Quinn sighed. "Lassie, do I have to spell everything out to a smart one like you? My gals know I'm batting a thousand with the rentals here and want to take a look at the new tenants for themselves…to see if they should bet against me."

"Have you got money riding on this nonsense?" asked Logan.

"I've got something more important," replied Quinn. "My reputation."

##

Bart Quinn closed the door behind him with a little snap. If he left it up to the young people themselves, they'd let opportunities fly away. He scanned the street as he walked down the front steps. A smile bloomed when he spotted a longtime friend and her sidekick. Then he frowned and hurried to the sidewalk.

"Hello, Marie!" he said, "and little Bonnie. Taking in the fresh air, are you?" But the white cane with the red tip at the bottom was new, and a frisson of concern ran through him.

The woman turned her head toward his voice. "Bartholomew Quinn. Always good to see you, my dear."

"Same here. What kind of new tricks are you up to?"

She nodded toward the hand holding the cane. "I'm practicing with my new toy. And Bonnie's helping. Safety first, you know."

"Grandma can walk faster now," said Bonnie. "And she goes outside more."

"Always good to breathe the fresh air," said Bart.

Bonnie nodded so hard her hair flew in a cloud around her. "Oh, yes. Now I can go outside more, too!"

Bart winced at the flash of pain crossing Marie's face. As Bonnie's legal guardian, his friend had some tough challenges ahead. Tragically, there was no mom or dad. But every little child should be able to play outside.

"You're a very good girl." Bart leaned toward the child. "So tell me, how do you like going to school on a bus?"

Her blue eyes shone with excitement. "Ooh, I love school. I love Ms. MacKenzie. She's so fun and tells good stories and she combs my hair...and... fixes my sweater...oh, oh...and look, Mr. Quinn. There she is."

She whirled toward Marie. "Grandma, Grandma, there's my teacher!"

From the excitement in Bonnie's voice and her wide smile, Joy MacKenzie could have been a movie star. Or a rock star. Maybe she was both in Bonnie's eyes. Bart refocused his attention on Marie, who was turning her head from side to side.

"On your left, Marie. Bonnie's teacher is walking down the path from Sea View House to the sidewalk. She always wears bright colors—today it's sky blue. The gal has high energy and a warm heart. Perfect match for your Bonnie."

Marie nodded. "I felt the same at Meet the Teacher Day last spring. Ms. MacKenzie had lots of ideas and enthusiasm, and I knew Bonnie would be in good hands." Her words faded and Bart patted her arm.

"We'll talk again soon, Marie. Now here comes Joy to say hello."

He watched the two women greet each other, delighted that Joy seemed comfortable chatting with Marie. Totally unselfconscious. He caught phrases like, "Call me Marie," and stepped closer to listen to the conversation.

"Bonnie pays excellent attention. She especially loves story time. She says her grandma tells the best stories ever."

Marie chuckled. "That's because her grandma taught English for over thirty years. I've devoured more than a few stories in my life."

"Here's an idea for you," said Joy. "Maybe you can volunteer to be our 'mystery reader' one day. I've set it up as a surprise. Parents come in and read to the class, but not even their own child knows which day it will be. Ergo, mystery reader."

"Very imaginative," said Bart. "Gets everyone involved."

"Hmm...I like that part," said Marie. "I guess I'll be the 'mystery storyteller' when my turn comes." She paused a moment. "Maybe...with puppets."

Joy beamed. "Wow. That's a fantastic idea, and the children will love it. We'll set a date, and I'll get someone to give you a ride...maybe my downstairs neighbor."

"You mean that nice Logan?" asked Marie. "He did deliver the pictures he took at the sand sculpture contest just like he promised. When I put them under my magnifying light, I thought he made us look beautiful. I framed the best one so Bonnie can see it at anytime."

Bart took in the scene, one person at a time, each individual trying to make her way, figure things out. His gut feeling about people went into overdrive.

"Marie, I hope you and Bonnie are free for dinner this Friday night. I'm having a little party at The Lobster Pot, and your favorite teacher and photographer will be there. Say you'll join us, and I'll pick you up early."

He felt her hesitate and held his breath.

"Oh...I-I don't know...it's been a long time. I always loved your daughters' cooking when I used to eat out, and the company would be a treat, but a restaurant?" She tapped her mouth. "I just don't know."

Bonnie tilted her head back. "Grandma? What's a restaurant?"

And with that one question, Bart witnessed a transformation in his reluctant friend. Her jaw lifted, her lips compressed, and her nostrils flared. Her free hand fisted at her side.

"I've made up my mind, Bartholomew, and thank you. Bonnie and I would be delighted to have dinner with you and your family...and entourage."

"Bravo," he muttered.

"Bravo, my foot," she whispered. "I could embarrass you, but I'll take my chances."

He looked from Marie to her granddaughter and thought of his own children, grandchildren, and great-grandchildren. His heart filled.

"It's all about Bonnie," he said.

"Of course, it's about my granddaughter. I'd do anything for her, anything to provide for her health and happiness. I'm not young anymore." The quiver in her voice revealed all.

"Grandma!" shouted Bonnie. "A big dog's coming out of the house. This is the best day ever."

Marie swung toward her granddaughter's voice. "Bart, is the dog well behaved?"

"Perfect. Heeling next to Logan."

Her eyes filled. "Damn my poor vision and my age. Bonnie needs more than I can give her."

Bart winced in agreement. He could do just so much arranging. Even with the fine people in residence, this particular child needed more magic than Sea View House could provide.

##

Logan licked the envelope, stamped it, and set it on the kitchen counter, ready to mail the next morning. Seeing Marie Oakley and Bonnie earlier had reminded him of Tommy's grandparents. He'd wanted to send them a picture of Ajax's retirement from the military, had mentioned it to the captain at the base. Now Tommy's folks would have a record of their grandson's buddy in the field. They'd know for sure that Tommy hadn't been alone.

Since his move to Sea View House, he hadn't been alone, either. He'd wanted his privacy, had demanded it from Quinn. But somehow the image of Joy MacKenzie followed him everywhere. He'd made a friend in Adam Fielding and gotten involved with Marie and Bonnie

Oakley, the staff at the diner, and the ROMEOs. A bunch of young moms knew who he was because of his camera. He scratched his head. In two weeks, he knew more people in Pilgrim Cove than he knew after five years in his Boston apartment building. Not that he'd exactly lived there all that time, but it was a home base.

Joy. He reached for his cell phone, then stopped. Memories of a fantastic kiss lingered, but pursuing the woman upstairs was dangerous, not part of his plan. His solitary life was comfortable and safe, with no complications. Joy would definitely be a complication. She was innocent with a tender heart and cared too much about everyone. She was meant for a real relationship. Husband. Family. The whole enchilada.

He didn't know how a real family worked. No family had wanted him, not even his own. But Joy tempted him. Too bad she wasn't the type for a quick hookup. He'd been with enough women to know the difference and made a practice of avoiding the vulnerable ones, the ones who'd get hurt. He wanted a clear conscience.

A knock on the door interrupted his thoughts. Jax trotted over, tail wagging. With a quick pull on the knob, Logan wasn't surprised to see Joy on the threshold.

"Want to go for a walk?" she asked while rubbing the dog behind the ears. "You can turn this baby loose on the beach now. Summer rules are over."

He grabbed his camera. "A fading sun. Good idea."

"Really? It's kind of dark out there."

"That's the point. The light's always changing. Let's find out what the lens can see."

He'd been taking some candid shots for the last few days as he'd walked miles of sidewalks, roads, and beaches. People, pets, nature. The town was a microcosm of America, and he wanted the place to seep into his bones. As the outsider, his objectivity would insure pictures that revealed truth. The goal of every professional photographer. He felt at home with a camera and grateful for discovering photography while still young. Grateful, in hindsight, for the teachers who'd encouraged him. Not that he stayed in touch.

He'd keep noodling around and see if any worthy projects presented themselves. A lot to explore, and nothing would appear the same twice.

"That's interesting," said Joy, stepping ahead of him as he closed the door. "I thought you needed time to set up a shot before you took it."

"I try to be fast because there are always surprises. That's what really makes it interesting."

High tide kept them close to big dunes separating the beach from the road. As they walked, the pale rays of sun wove a pattern of light and dark across the sand.

Logan paused. Looked through his lens and kneeled. "The contrast's perfect." *Click, whirr*. He turned toward Joy and caught his breath. The fading light touched her from behind, creating a glow all around her. Shimmering, stunning, highlighting the shades of blue she wore, as artful as any stained glass her mother could create.

Click. Click. Again. He'd never get tired of shooting her.

"I found some sea glass." Joy stepped to the right and bent down.

"Like a ballerina," he whispered, captured by her grace and capturing it with his camera.

She straightened and held out her prize. "Put that thing down, and look at this great piece."

"Hold it against your palm. We'll document it." He took a shot of the frosted-looking green glass, smoothed from weathering. Then she carefully slipped it into her pocket and hugged Ajax. His camera never stopped.

"Come on, boy. Let's run." She took a step, Ajax looked back at him, and he motioned the dog to go.

He watched them through the Nikon's lens, taking one shot after another as they set off. Focusing intently on his subjects, he knew the exact moment when the remaining fingers of sunlight disappeared. The exact moment he lost sight of Joy, and the exact moment he was alone. In the pitch dark. On a deserted beach. Another unfamiliar place. Memory stirred. More distant than Iraq and Afghanistan. A long-ago remembrance that made him shiver. He inhaled deeply, then exhaled. He wasn't a child hiding in a closet anymore. Bury it!

"Hey, Logan. Aren't you coming with us?" Joy's cheerful voice cut through the dark and cut his musing short. The sand stopped shifting. Once more, he stood on solid ground.

CHAPTER SEVEN

Wearing a long black dress with batik-style copper print, Joy leaned toward the bathroom mirror and inserted her second shell earring. She stepped back to evaluate. Good, but not complete. She knew what was missing. Soon she placed a shell pendant, hanging on strands of tiny metallic seed beads, around her neck. Perfect…and her own work, with materials donated by her mom. Smiling, she slipped her feet into wedge sandals, selected an airy crocheted shawl, and headed for the kitchen.

Because of Bart Quinn's invitation to them both, she wouldn't call dinner at the Lobster Pot an actual date with Logan—although he seemed to take it seriously. He'd waited for her on the porch when she'd returned from work that afternoon to check the plan.

"Walk or ride?" he asked.

"Walk. Definitely. While the weather's still good. If this were December…I'd give you a different answer."

"December? I'll be gone by then. In fact, we'll both be out of here before Christmas."

Her heart squeezed for a moment. "I suppose so."

"If I pick you up at five thirty," said Logan, "we'll arrive before six."

"Pick me up?" she asked. "I can meet you outside in the driveway."

He studied her in silence. "Not going to happen. We're walking there together, and I'll call for you at your door...your upstairs door."

She hadn't argued the point further. If he wanted to act the protector on the safe streets of Pilgrim Cove, fine. Maybe military manners had seeped inside him while he'd been embedded with the troops.

His knock came precisely at five thirty, just as she reached the kitchen. She opened the door and stared. The man was gorgeous. Clean shaven with a hint of a smile that reached his eyes.

"You clean up really well," she said, swallowing hard. The sleeves of his powder-blue shirt were pushed to the elbows and paired with black slacks and loafers.

"Ditto," he said softly. His glance swept over her, his eyes changing from bright silver to dark smoky. He reached for her arm. "Ready?"

More than ready. But for what?

They reached the Lobster Pot in no time. At least, that was the impression Joy had of their walk along Outlook Drive and Main Street. Conversation never lagged, from her day with the kids to his day with Ajax and camera.

"But no camera this evening?" she asked.

"Not necessary. Tonight I'll depend on my own eyes. No extra lenses. No filters."

"At the Lobster Pot, you should depend on your nose and taste buds."

They walked up the two steps of the restaurant's deep wraparound porch. When Logan opened the door, the most delicious aromas ever to hit her olfactory glands wafted to them. Joy's stomach rumbled.

"I must be starving," she said with a laugh.

"Then you've come to the right place. And right on time." Bart Quinn ushered them in as though he'd been waiting for long-lost cousins. "We've got three separate eating areas, but tonight we'll be in the main dining room." He led them down the corridor as he spoke.

Wood paneling covered the walls. In the dining room hung framed colorful posters with nautical themes, some artistic, but most with corny captions beneath. "Oh, my. Look at that one," said Joy, slowing down to point at a poster with two boys in a rowboat. The caption said, "Wouldn't you rudder be fishing?"

"I don't know whether to laugh or cry," whispered Logan into her ear. "Very punny."

"Ouch. Now look over there." Joy pointed to a poster of a Pilgrim Cove map which proclaimed Pilgrim Cove as a "Hull of a place to live." "In case you're wondering, Bart's daughters come up with these," explained Joy. "So keep your real thoughts to yourself."

"My lips are sealed."

"Good move. You'll appreciate that they cook better than they write."

"The posters may be sort of silly," said Logan, slowly looking around, "but I like them. Put all together, they celebrate the town—the women's hometown—and the people in it. It must have taken time to create the art and think up the captions. Bart's daughters…care. They love the place."

Of course, he was right. She squeezed his hand. "I agree. Totally."

Bart led them to a large round table in the center of the room. Marie and Bonnie were already seated next to two young girls who held Bonnie in their spell. The child had eyes only for the "big" girls.

"I've already met Sara," said Logan. "Adam's daughter. She wants to be a vet like her dad."

"The other girl is her best friend and Bart's great-granddaughter, Katie Parker," said Joy, "Her folks are the ones with the new...b-baby." She heard her voice catch and rushed the introductions. The surprise of seeing Lila and Jason Parker out with their three-month-old left no time to build her defenses. She took a breath and forced herself to smile. To *ooh* and *aah*. And then to greet Rachel and Jack Levine with relief until she noticed Rachel's baby bump. The high school's assistant principal would be asking for maternity leave soon.

"Seems the town's having a population explosion," Joy said, glad her voice remained steady. She slipped into the chair next to Marie.

Her tablemates chuckled, but she felt Logan's hand squeeze hers. "Something wrong?" he whispered as he nodded to the others.

Just everything. Most women had babies, and she'd have to accept that she wouldn't. Taking a deep breath, she pictured Glory getting into character, and tried to borrow her sister's technique. She gathered happy thoughts. Morning meetings with the kids. Building sand castles. Kissing Logan.

Her cheeks heated. She knew they turned pink, but she looked at Logan anyway. "I'm fine," she said. "Having a wonderful time."

A frown crossed his face. "I hope so. These are *your* friends and neighbors."

"They're yours, too."

He didn't respond for a moment but then said, "That's true...for now."

The last two words made her breathless for the second time in a few moments. The evening was quickly going downhill.

Until Bonnie spotted her, jumped from her seat, and, calling "Miss Joy, Miss Joy," ran right into her arms.

##

"I called her Bouncing Bonnie this evening. She couldn't contain her excitement, knowing you'd be here tonight," said Marie.

Joy gave the woman her full attention. The dark glasses protected Marie's eyes from the glare of lights indoors, from the glare of the sun outdoors. But it also partially hid Marie's facial expression, and Joy focused on trying to anticipate her needs and help her. She shouldn't have bothered. Marie's matter-of-fact manner about her disability put Joy at ease almost immediately. Soon she realized Marie's attitude could be one Joy should emulate regarding her own disappointment.

"Bonnie is a wonderful girl," said Joy. "She makes friends easily. And she's smart, in fact, exceptionally verbal. Her vocabulary is astounding for her age."

To her horror, Joy saw tears roll from beneath the dark glasses. She clasped the woman's hand. "Please don't cry, Marie. Your granddaughter loves school, and she'll do well."

The woman quickly wiped her face. "Of course, of course. And thank you. Don't mind me. I'm just a silly old woman." Marie got her bearings and turned toward Bart, on her other side. "We'll talk to her after dinner, Bartholomew?" Her whisper was loud enough to reach Joy.

"I promise," replied Bart.

Uh-oh. Joy had no idea what to expect from these two longtime friends, but one thing she did know. Marie Oakley was not a silly old woman.

Almost two hours later, Logan's appetite had been so satisfied he couldn't imagine any of Bart's guests eating another morsel for a week. "Delicious and thank you, Bart," he said, patting his stomach.

"My daughters have done it again," boasted Quinn. "You can't move, can you?"

Everyone laughed, groaned, and began making their way from the room. But not before Jack Levine, a marine biologist, and his wife, Rachel, pointed out "their" customized poster Maggie and Thea had come up with:

Jack *floundered* around the seven seas,

Till Rachel said, "He's my *Maine* squeeze."

"Now that one is really clever," said Logan, "assuming Jack comes from the Pine Tree state."

"I'm definitely a native," said the man in question. "From outside of Portland, along the coast. I spent my youth in a lobster boat."

"And he hasn't become a landlubber yet," laughed his wife. "Which is fine. We both love being out on the water."

"Nice," said Logan.

"Nice?" echoed Quinn. "Only nice? Why, Jack and Rachel are a perfect match! Thanks to Sea View House and yours truly. And what about Becca and Adam? Same thing." He pointed a finger at Logan and tapped him on the chest. "Let the magic come in, boy. Let it in."

A ribbon of impatience ran through Logan. The old guy never gave up. A sentimental romantic, something that Logan would never be and couldn't even understand. He liked Joy—a lot. Would love to kiss her breathless and make everlasting love to her. The mere thought of it made him erect, for crying out loud. But in the end, he wouldn't want to hurt her. She was too sweet, too naïve and innocent. Too protected by her family and this town.

He glanced at Quinn, who was now speaking to Marie. He heard the old man say, "Let's talk with Joy, and then I'll take you and the little one home."

Logan stepped back, content to watch his neighbors and wait for Joy. He saw the group mingle and reassemble into smaller groups, like in a square dance or a minuet. He took it all in, an observer, standing comfortably. Standing near but on the outside, not part of the group. Even with the army, he'd been attached to a unit but not a member of it. There was a big difference. He understood his function, was used to it, and normally had no problem. Tonight, however, he did.

Tonight's social activity was more complicated for him than any military operation. Regimentation vs. flexibility. In this local hangout with friendly people, he wasn't on assignment, didn't have a mission. He'd been invited here. Welcomed in. He didn't get it and didn't quite know how to act. Where he fit.

He missed his camera. Maybe that was it. He should have taken the small Nikon and gone to work. Earlier, he'd seen Marie trace the top edge of her soup bowl and carefully spoon the chowder to her mouth. He'd observed little Bonnie basking in the attention of the older girls. People were interesting. Their expressions revealed stories. Searching the faces of his companions and watching their body language, he could have written a slew of stories about this small town at the water's edge. His thoughts raced until…Life at the Water's Edge.

He could include the ocean in all its moods and the marine life it supported. The beach with its offerings— the shells, sea glass, and sea grass. But most important, life at the water's edge meant the folks who lived there, who chose to live there. And those who might not have much choice. He tucked his ideas away—a self-imposed assignment—and relaxed, once more comfortable in his own skin.

Joy reappeared, startling him from his musings. She looked wonderful. Her eyes shone bright blue, her smile wide and warm as though she hadn't seen him in months. Despite the big meal, her energy was as high as when they'd started the evening.

"Hey," he said, reaching for her hand. "Ready to go?" He looked forward to walking home together, kissing her at the door, and seeing what happened next.

"Just getting my wrap." She quickly arranged the shawl and tilted her head back to see him. "I've got something to tell you." Excitement laced her voice; her eyes shone.

"Something good?"

"Very good. Let's go and I'll reveal all."

The definition of good would have to be debated. A good deed might be a better description, and no good deed ever went unpunished. A verifiable cliché. He didn't like surprises and hadn't reacted immediately to her announcement in word or deed. Through the years, he'd trained himself to wait and learn more, to count to three. He found it hard, however, to follow the rules this time. He wanted to shout. He wanted to shake sense into her. Instead, he took a deep breath.

"So, let me get this straight," he began. "You've agreed to take the little girl in to live with you for an entire month. Have I got that right?"

"Yes. That's how long Marie expects to be away at school. It'll be fun. I can teach her colors—she hasn't quite got them down yet. And as Marie said, she wants Bonnie to be around younger people."

Her fingers pressed his forearm, and his skin burned. He reminded himself to focus. "Is there no one else?" he asked. "No other family? An aunt, another grandma, someone besides you?"

"No one. Her parents died in a car accident three years ago. Marie's her legal guardian." She pulled away and faced him. "It's a simple arrangement. Why are you asking so many questions?"

Naïve. So naïve. Nothing was ever simple, especially with people. Especially with families.

"Oh, no!" Joy cried, pulling away before he could reply. "Please don't tell me you're upset because Bonnie will be at Sea View House, maybe making noise and invading your privacy."

Stunned, he put up his hands like a traffic cop. "Whoa! If that's what you think of me, get it out of your head right now." A kaleidoscope of blended memories ran through his mind like a newsreel. All dark and cloudy. All bad. He would have promised anything to live in Sea View House with a nice mom when he'd been a child.

Joy stepped forward again, stroked his face, his temple. "I'm sorry to upset you. I thought you liked Bonnie, but you're acting so…so…negative."

He covered her hand, still on his cheek, slowly brought it to his lips. Kissed it. "You're going to get hurt." His gut twisted at the thought. His housemate needed a keeper. Just when he'd started to admit he was wrong about her, that she wasn't as ditzy as he'd assumed, she committed to something as serious as childcare without thinking twice. She was a gentle person, a butterfly, flitting from flower to flower. Ajax could teach her a few things, like how to be focused and tough.

"What happens at the end of the month," he asked, "when Marie returns from that special school? What happens then?"

She pulled ahead of him and turned back. "What do you mean? Bonnie will return to her grandmother. The arrangement's just temporary. And it makes sense."

"Maybe on paper," he said, leading her down their driveway. "But nothing's ever that simple."

##

Including a kiss. A kiss was not simple, not when Joy's mind, filled with plans for Bonnie, suddenly went blank. When Logan's lips brushed hers, all thought disappeared. The taste, touch, warmth of his mouth—delicious. She breathed him in and pulled him closer as naturally as if she'd been doing it forever.

The tingling in her body surprised her. Pleasure radiated outward from deep inside, and her heartbeat quickened. His tongue entered her mouth, and she wanted more. She heard herself moan, sensed his wanting, before reality stepped in, and she stepped back. And stared.

He seemed no better than she. His face was taut, lips rigid. And his eyes as dark as midnight. It had all happened so fast.

"Logan…?"

"Hmm?"

"I-I…what's hap…uh, we need to—"

"I've got to walk the dog."

"Oh. Sure." Just as well. She inserted her key in the lock but couldn't resist a parting word. "Coward."

He didn't flinch. "You'd be, too, if you gave it some thought. Life can get…complicated."

"Ahh. So that's it. Afraid of getting too involved." She inclined her head to the side and hoped her smile was natural. "For the record—we're standing in mutual territory. I plan on remaining single for the rest of my life."

His lips parted, his eyebrows hit his hairline. "You? The goddess of home and hearth and needlepoint? Who loves every kid in your class, even though you just met them two days ago? You don't have to lie to me, Joy. And I won't lie to you."

She could have reassured him right then of his freedom. But he'd ignited her curiosity, and he seemed to have more to say.

"I like you," he began. "And, obviously, you turn me on. But there's no long-term anything with me." He shrugged. "Being a rolling stone fits me well. So I won't kiss you again, and I'll stay away if that's what you want."

She met his eyes with a steadfast gaze. "Listen up, Logan. I'm not lying. I have no intention to ever marry or have a family." And she discovered that repeating her new plan—believing her new plan—became easier the more often she said it aloud. "So, you're safe. There won't be any complications." She turned the knob. "And by the way, I like you, too."

She left him then. Ran upstairs to her apartment, wondering how long it would take before they became friends with benefits. It would be a perfect relationship and temporary by definition. The thought pleased her. It should please Logan, too.

##

Logan unleashed Jax and watched him take off across the hard-packed sand. As usual, the dog didn't go too far before pausing to wait for his man.

"Good boy. Good boy." He rubbed Jax's neck, heaping praise on him. It was only at night, with no pedestrians around, that he gave the dog his freedom. Usually he and Jax paced each other, but tonight Logan was still digesting the delicious meal he'd recently consumed. Walking would suit him fine. Walking and thinking went well together.

Joy was hiding something. Had to be. If Logan hadn't basked in the warmth of her smile, observed her natural interaction with kids and her friendliness with everyone she met, he might have believed her. If he knew less about her, he could have bought into her assertion. No marriage, no family. He didn't believe a word. None of it made sense.

"What have you got there?"

Ajax deposited a plastic shovel at Logan's feet. "Okay, boy. Want to fetch?" He threw the toy and watched with pride as Jax retrieved it in seconds and dropped it at Logan's feet once more. The shepherd's tail wagged—oh, he was proud of himself—then he stood on his hind legs, front paws on Logan's chest.

"You missed me, did you? Likely story. You probably slept all evening." He received a lick on the cheek and laughed. "You're a good boy."

He'd kept Jax in great mental and physical shape, heaped him with affection, and spent hours with him walking around town. Many people had become regulars in the meet-and-greet arena. As Logan played with Jax on the beach that night and received his slobbering kisses, his last doubt disappeared. He was definitely the right person to have adopted this four-legged hero. Maybe the military would label him as Jax's new handler, but he knew he was more than that—more like a dad. Or how he thought a dad would feel. He loved his "boy."

So Joy had been right in the beginning. He and Jax had become a family, and somehow he was okay with it. More than okay. If he could love Jax as much as he did, he knew he could love a little boy or girl. There was nothing wrong with him. His childhood hadn't scarred him for life, and he was just like other men with families. Not that he wanted to change his single status and his lifestyle. He and Jax were a complete unit.

But as for Joy? He couldn't imagine her not wanting a child of her own. He shrugged. What did he know? He sure wasn't an expert on females. Far from it. Maybe her attitude had something to do with having a challenging profession. Maybe she was choosing a career over family.

One day, he'd find out the truth. Maybe.

CHAPTER EIGHT

On Friday afternoon a week later, Joy met Marie in her lawyer's office and signed the agreement making her Bonnie's temporary guardian for a period of up to sixty days, the number generally allowed by law. Copies would go to the school and Bonnie's pediatrician. Joy watched Marie write her name, not surprised the older woman had a method of following the edge of a ruler to create a straight signature. When Joy had visited Marie and Bonnie at their home earlier in the week, she'd learned just how carefully Bonnie's grandma made her way in the world.

"I'm not totally blind, but what vision I have is pretty poor. So everything in the house has a place and is put back in its place after being used. I invented little tricks to help me." She gestured toward the television. "Notice the piece of Velcro taped to the on button so I can feel where it is."

"It makes perfect sense." The large house was not only immaculate but explained why Bonnie insisted her classmates put all items away exactly as they'd found them in their appropriate activity corners.

"Grandma figures things out," said Bonnie. "She can't see good, but she's smart."

"The correct word is *well*, pumpkin. I can't see well. It's an adverb. *Good* is an adjective."

Bonnie wrinkled her nose and sighed. "I forgot." She peeked at Joy, then back at her grandmother. "We don't do proper English in kindergarten, do we Ms. MacKenzie?"

Not with the grammatical explanations of good and well. "We certainly do speak correctly in kindergarten." Joy kneeled in front of the girl. "Every day in school, we say 'good morning,' not 'well morning.' Don't we?"

Bonnie started to giggle. "That sounds so funny— well morning."

"I can't read to her anymore," said Marie. "I don't even know Braille writing, but I have hundreds of stories up here." She pointed at her forehead. "I can retrieve one from a file cabinet in my mind. I suppose teaching English prepared me well. Bonnie and I have lots of story discussions."

Bonnie nodded vigorously. "We guess about what happens next."

"But now I have to learn other things. Computers. Technology. That's part of what I'm going to learn at school. There are lots of adaptive devices that can help me." The woman spoke bravely, but Joy detected a tremble in her voice.

"Computers are not as hard as you think, and I'm sure the teachers will be excellent."

"I'm sure, too, but I'm not young, my dear. Everything is a challenge."

"Heck, Marie. You're no older than Bart Quinn, and let's face it, nothing stops him!"

She must have tickled Marie's funny bone, because the woman's fear turned into mirth. "So true. Bartholomew is one of a kind and an inspiration." In a moment, however, her demeanor changed back again. "But even a good friend like Bart cannot imagine how concerned I am about the future. So thank you for taking Bonnie, not only for my sake but for hers. She'll have fun with you."

She squeezed Marie's hand. "Bonnie is an awesome child."

Now Marie's smile could have warmed the world. "Well,*I* think so. But *child* is the key word. Is she like others her age? As playful? She worries about me. She has too much responsibility." Her eyes filled. "It's just not fair to her, not fair to any of us."

She'd hit Joy's vulnerable spot, and Joy's heart tore. "I-I guess there's no such thing as fair, Marie, but we deal with it. We learn to deal with it."

"Of course we do. Don't mind me. I'm just feeling sorry for myself."

But Joy hadn't often met a braver person than Marie Oakley. If she needed a moment to grieve for what might have been, so be it. "I'll do my best with Bonnie."

"I don't think it will be too hard," replied Marie, a smile now blossoming. "She can't stop talking about school and Ms. MacKenzie. She's very excited about her visit. She loves you already."

##

In the lawyer's office, Joy folded her copies of the agreement, took the lawyer's business card, and tucked everything into her tote bag. Standing, she, Marie, and Bonnie prepared to leave. "Ready to visit the Crow's Nest?"

Bonnie's eyes grew bigger than bicycle wheels. "A nest? Do we fly there?"

"Even Ms. MacKenzie can't do that," said Marie.

"Oh, yes, she can," insisted Bonnie. "She makes Richard and Marc stay quiet in school, and they are *so* noisy, and they make a mess. So she can do anything. Maybe it's magic." She turned to Joy. "Do you snap your fingers and say 'Presto, chango,' and poof! They listen?"

The child was precious and adorable, with an outstanding imagination. "Sorry, Bonnie. No finger snapping. But maybe the magic is that the boys are learning. They're settling down."

Dusk had fallen by the time she drove back to Sea View House with her charges. This visit was for Marie's sake. The woman, so devoted to her granddaughter, would be gone for a month. She wanted to take away an impression of Bonnie's new environment.

As they got out of the car, Joy said, "You'll stay for supper. I've made meatballs—my mom's recipe—and we'll boil up some spaghetti. How does that sound?"

"It sounds like too much trouble for you," said Marie.

"Not at all. I want you to feel comfortable." She glanced at the disappearing Bonnie. "Your granddaughter is racing down the driveway to my door. I guess her feeling comfortable is not an issue."

At that moment, Joy glimpsed a four-legged shadow and laughed at herself. It wasn't Joy's apartment that had caught Bonnie's attention. The child called out to them. "Look, look. Ajax is here. Ajax is here."

The dog and Logan appeared from the backyard. "We heard voices," said Logan, walking toward the car. "Hi, Ms. Oakley. Nice to see you again."

She extended her arm, and Logan stepped closer to take her hand. "Same here," said Marie. "I was hoping we'd run into each other before I left on this trip." Marie inclined her head. "Joy?"

"Here I am."

"Do you have enough meatballs and spaghetti for one more guest?"

Joy startled. Marie wasn't the type to force a situation. But this was no ordinary situation. A mother lion was protecting its cub. From the set of Marie's jaw, Grandma wasn't going anywhere without first checking out the details of Sea View House, despite the assurances Bart must have given her.

Under Marie's gentle questioning over dinner, Logan had revealed more about his professional life than Joy had known to ask. He'd traveled to Africa, capturing photographs of native wildlife, both safe and endangered. He'd done an in-depth piece on Alaska's salmon industry. His stories had been published in *National Geo*, *Reader's Digest*, and other major magazines.

"If it weren't for my high school art teachers, I'd be nowhere," he said. "So you all have my deepest respect and gratitude. You remind me of them."

"How did they help?" asked Marie. "I'm curious."

"Simple," said Logan. "They believed in me. The other kids thought I was weird with my drawings and cartoons. And I thought they needed an attitude adjustment. But, then again, I was the one who always got into trouble. I-I didn't fit in anywhere. A pencil was my best friend, but I was working on instinct. I didn't really know what I was doing. And then I walked into Mrs. Maggio's art class, and within two lessons, I had a mentor."

"She must be proud of you," said Marie.

He nodded. "I think she was, but she's gone now." His voice was a rasp. "Sh-she died when I was a senior."

And Joy remembered how he'd once said, "Everyone leaves." She squeezed his hand. "I'm sorry, Logan, but I'm glad you had her."

"The future lies ahead," said Marie. "Do not live in the past or you're done for. You must storm ahead and choose life!"

Joy felt herself sit straighter in her chair. Even Logan's eyes had widened.

"I can't forget Mrs. Maggio," he said, "but the past is behind me."

Did he really believe that? "The past is with all of us," said Joy.

He shot a pointed glance at her and addressed Marie. "I've forged my own career," Logan continued. "Either I take assignments from editors or I come up with my own stories…and shop them. I think I have a new one percolating inside my head." He paused, nodded. "Actually, a couple. But I'm not talking."

So he'd be traveling again. "You've just gotten to Sea View House," said Joy. "I thought you were taking a long break."

"I am. Fewer nightmares now, so that's progress. And new ideas are coming again. Maybe Bart's magic is the mix of ocean, sand, and sky."

"Not to mention Ajax," said Joy.

He held her gaze. "Right. And then there's the magpie."

"Oh, goodness, Logan. Stop teasing. If I didn't chat, we'd be living in silence."

Marie angled her head. "Perfect. I'm so glad that you two have a friendly relationship," she said. "Two are better than one, and I know Bonnie will be in very good hands."

"No, no, Marie," said Joy immediately. "You misunderstand. Logan may be up and gone tomorrow. You heard him. New ideas and all. This arrangement is just between you, Bonnie, and me."

"I know that, honey. And I have full confidence in you. I can go away with a peaceful mind."

"Good. Just don't leave with any false impressions."

Logan remained silent, but Bonnie filled the void.

"Logan, look. Get your camera. Look over there." With a jerk of her arm, she pointed to the living picture of a parakeet riding on the back of a German shepherd.

"For crying out loud," Logan grumbled. "Now it's not just sand sculpture. What a traitor."

"Never mind," said Joy. "I'll take a picture." She grabbed her cell phone and clicked away. "Bonnie, you get next to Ajax, too. I'll send this to Grandma's computer."

Logan's hands gently pushed her aside. "Out of the way, magpie. You'll send garbage with that thing."

She watched while he went to work. Squatting, standing, leaning, sitting, he missed no angle capturing the child and the pets. His brow furrowed and smoothed; his mouth tightened and relaxed. He worked hard, not for fame and glory or a prize story but because he cared. Marie deserved the best that was in him, and he wanted to make her happy.

Logan might have chosen a solitary life, but he wasn't a solitary man. He wasn't a loner. If anything, he hungered for connections. Joy saw that now, even if he didn't. She watched him tease Bonnie, get Jax to cooperate, and even coach Marie into posing for the camera. He emanated warmth and, at the moment, was the sun around which they all orbited.

He was wonderful. Absolutely wonderful. Loving and kind and strong— qualities she'd always admired. As she continued to watch him, a frisson of awareness danced through her, and she knew she was heading for trouble.

Loving Logan had not been in her game plan at all.

##

Logan turned the porch light on and, with Jax, sat on the front steps waiting for Joy. She was taking too long to drive her guests home. From the neck of the peninsula to Lookout Point, the entire length of land was only six miles. Marie lived about halfway. His fingers tapped his cell phone, but he cautioned himself to have patience. This was Pilgrim Cove, not Afghanistan. In a cozy small town, everyone knew everyone else, and no one planted IEDs.

Not five minutes later, he began pacing. The hell with it. Too bad if she didn't like him tracking her down. He punched in her number.

"Where are you?" he asked as soon as she picked up.

"What's wrong? What happened? I'm almost home."

He exhaled a deep breath, a breath he hadn't been aware of holding. "Nothing's wrong now. See you soon."

Dots of perspiration covered him. A slight nausea threatened. He recognized the symptoms, had experienced them when he'd been embedded with Tommy's unit. And he'd hated knowing what it represented.

Fear.

Jax was sniffing the ground. His pal was back in search mode. Not good. Get a grip. Get a grip. Joy wasn't out on a sortie. She was simply driving a neighbor home.

He sat back down and leaned against the higher steps. "Come on, boy. It's all right." Jax trotted over and laid his head in Logan's lap. "It's all right," Logan repeated. "I just had a little moment, but it's over."

Headlights appeared on the corner, and Logan watched Joy pull into the driveway. Safe and sound. "Idiot. I am an idiot." Jax licked him.

"Now you'll earn your dinner," said Joy, getting out of the car and opening the trunk. "Come help me carry this stuff upstairs."

"Stuff" was an understatement. "What is all this?" he asked, looking at several cartons.

"Bonnie's things. Toys, clothes, games, and books. And blankets."

"Blankets? This house is like a hotel. It came equipped with blankets and linen. Nice and clean, too."

She looked at him, shook her head. "Ah, Logan, Logan, Logan. These blankets aren't just any blankets, they're Bonnie's blankets. And therein lies the difference."

"I'll have to take your word." He didn't get it. "I would've been happy with any old warm cover when I was a kid."

"I'm so sorry, Logan," she said, stepping closer and squeezing his arm. "I guess you didn't have much."

The sorrow in her eyes almost overwhelmed him. The woman had too much heart and needed to be protected from the world. He cupped her face in his hands. "I'm fine now. Don't think about it." He lowered his head, brushed his mouth over her lips, and heard her intake of breath. He slowly increased the pressure. "You can think about that instead," he whispered a moment later.

Her lids slowly lifted. A sweet smile formed. Warm and beautiful. And directed at him. He forgot to breathe. The shadows he carried inside his heart disappeared, and it felt wonderful. But weird. Perhaps this was happiness…? Or even…something more?

"Oh, my. You're good, and you did give me something to think about," she said. "But that doesn't get you out of work. Grab a carton."

With a lighthearted laugh, he complied. Why had he ever thought she was an unfocused, easily distracted woman? Tonight, at least, Joy would not be deterred and, in his mind, could do no wrong.

He hoisted one carton on his shoulder and another under his opposite arm. By the weight of them, Bonnie hadn't left anything behind. Either everything the child owned must be important, or she thought she was moving in forever. He dismissed that idea as soon as it occurred. Bonnie would have some fun for a while, but she and her grandmother were a duo. Like bread and butter or mac and cheese. Besides, Sea View House was just a way station. A temporary fix for those needing a home. Like Joy. Like…him. Marie and Bonnie had a fine home. They weren't lost at all.

CHAPTER NINE

By Monday morning, Joy was ready to return to work. To her classroom routines. Running a kindergarten of eighteen children seemed easier than preparing for one child to live with her. Too much second-guessing. On Saturday afternoon, she'd finally called Marie to get a grocery list of Bonnie's favorite foods, find out about bedtime routines and a list of friends she could play with on weekends or after school. Details. Details. But Bonnie would arrive this Friday, and Joy had to be ready. Logan had laughed at her but disappeared for much of the time. Seemed he was exploring a new project.

But the evenings had been…more than nice, including another dinner at The Lobster Pot. Alone this time. But bumping into Adam and Rebecca Fielding and Sara. Later that night, they'd all met at the soccer field to give their dogs a chance to run. Sara's retired racer needed an enclosed environment, or as Sara explained, "she's a sight hound and could chase something and get hit by a car."

Who knew?

Today's morning meeting with the kids came and went, then number work and activity corner play. Time to plan for the apple orchard trip. Routines were well and good…for a while.

Choosing to eat lunch at her desk, she pulled out her cell phone to call the orchard but was startled at the knock at her door.

An older student, about Sara's age, stood there. "Ms. MacKenzie, you need to come to the office. The principal said so."

She couldn't question a child. Grabbing her purse, she followed the girl down the hall and into the general office. And saw Logan. He was beside her in two steps.

"What's wrong?"

"Marie's had an accident. Do you have that court order with you?"

The agreement? Where was the agreement? She riffled through her purse. "I'm looking." Yes. There it was. "Got it. What happened?"

"It was the damnedest thing. She tripped on the path between her house and the sidewalk. Jax and I saw everything. Marie was walking, and suddenly she was on the ground. Cane and all. And she was screaming." His mouth tightened, lips pressed flat against each other.

Joy winced."Oh, no. Poor Marie."

"The ambulance came within minutes," said Logan, "but she kept screaming and talking about Bonnie. Taking care of Bonnie. So I'm guessing the medics are gonna call Child Protective Services, and we've got to stop that."

He nodded toward the inner office. "Mrs. Cohen's waiting for us."

"You've spoken with her?"

"Well, Bart Quinn's at the hospital, the neighbors are packing a bag for Marie and locking up the house, so somebody had to come to school."

Somebody. The man who didn't want to get involved with anyone.

"Where's Jax?"

"Tied up outside. H-he wouldn't leave Marie until the medics came."

The morning had taken its toll on many. She grasped his hand and squeezed. "Let's go in."

Fifteen minutes later, a photocopy of Joy's guardianship order was filed with Mrs. Cohen. "This will do until the original arrives." She directed her attention to Joy. "It's hard to keep a professional distance from families when living in a small town. The staff who live out of town have an easier time. In this case, however, I'm happy Bonnie's guardian is local. I was concerned about her anyway."

"My tenure is for up to sixty days," said Joy.

"Then we have sixty days to figure out a real solution." The principal leaned across her desk. "My mother is almost blind, too. My siblings and I have to help her. She's as bright and determined as Bonnie's grandma, but managing her own life is her full-time job. My mom could never raise a child now. And neither can Marie. Nor should she have to—even if she hadn't had this fall."

"But they love—" Joy began and felt Logan's eyes on her before he interrupted.

"I suggest we take one step at a time. First off is to find out Marie's condition." He glanced at Joy. "Call Bart."

Her cell rang, and she checked the readout. "Great minds." She connected and listened, then spoke. "Tell Marie not to worry. Bonnie's with me. The school is in agreement, so all is well. Hang on." She turned to the others.

"She's got a broken right wrist and right leg. Bad, but at least it's not the hip. So that's good. She'll go directly to rehab from the hospital."

She spoke into the phone again. "When can I bring Bonnie to visit?"

A minute later, she hung up. "Surgery's tomorrow. We can visit in two days." Sighing, she added, "Marie never even made it to her school. She was so looking forward to it."

The principal shook her head. "There are services that teach independent living skills in the home. I wonder why Mrs. Oakley wanted to attend an out-of-town program."

To show Bonnie that she can survive without her. Joy said nothing. Instead, she rose, shook hands with her boss, and checked her watch. "I need to get back to the classroom."

"See you later," said Logan, standing alongside her.

"You and Jax…on the porch steps again?"

He held her gaze, eyes warming and turning hot. "Count on it."

"But *when* can I see Grandma?" Bonnie's words combined with sobs.

Joy glanced in her rearview mirror to check on her charge. Bonnie sat belted in the middle of the backseat, almost invisible. The child needed a car seat. Or at least a booster seat. Joy seemed to remember her nephews climbing into these contraptions. She'd call her brother later and find out.

"We'll visit Grandma in two days. The day after tomorrow."

Pause. "So that's Wednesday. Right?"

"Exactly."

"Promise?"

"Promise. But after school, sweetie. Grandma wouldn't like you to miss school. And I have to go to work, too."

Giggles. "Oh, Ms. Joy. You don't work! You play with us."

Right. "Look, Bonnie. Look who's waiting for us out front."

"I can't see," she wailed. "Who? Grandma?"

Joy's heart shredded for the little girl. Logic and reason went only so far with a five-year-old. "Not Grandma. Remember, she's in the hospital. But your big, furry friend is waiting."

"Ajax!" Joy heard the child's excitement and then her struggle with the seat belt. She had no experience manipulating safety latches.

"Wait a minute, Bonnie, and I'll help." She pulled into the driveway and got out. A minute later, she watched Bonnie run to her canine friend. Saw Logan speak quietly to both the child and the dog. But in the end, Bonnie's arms went around Ajax's neck while he sat tall and proud.

"Ajax may prove to be my strongest ally here," said Joy as she closed the space between her and Logan.

"Stronger than me?" His pained expression was laughable.

"Who's she hugging? You or the dog?"

"Which leaves my arms empty, waiting for you." Sincerity registered behind the joke, and she continued toward him, pressing her hand to his cheek. "So how was the rest of your day?" he asked.

She inclined her head toward the child. "It's not over yet, and I'm not sure she gets it."

"Nighttime is the worst. You'll have your hands full later."

"Monsters under the bed, huh?"

"Under the bed, in the closet, and everywhere else, too. In lots of disguises."

Maybe it was his voice or the dark hue of his eyes, but that frisson of awareness she sometimes felt with Logan crept down her spine and caused her to be still. "Logan?" she whispered.

"I speak from experience, but that's behind me." He looked past her shoulder, avoiding her eyes.

No, no. She wanted to howl. But all she could do was squeeze his arm. Pat his shoulder. Hug.

"It's all right, Joy. I'm fine." He stepped toward his own entrance. "You'll want time alone with Bonnie to settle her into the Crow's Nest. If you need anything, call me. You've got my number."

She sure did. His number was becoming clearer every day but would never rival the clarity of a sparkling windowpane. It would fit perfectly, however, in the world of stained glass. Beautiful but shaded. Perhaps to remain that way forever.

Not good enough! Not for Logan. "Like Marie said, 'don't live in the past.'"

He paused at the screen door. "I could say the same to you. Tell me, sweetheart, what causes the sadness in your eyes when you think no one's looking?"

Stunned. Gut punched. She'd hidden her secret so well—or so she'd thought. Copying Glory's art wasn't enough. She needed real acting lessons from her sister.

"Come on, Bonnie. Spread your fairy wings and fly upstairs with me."

Logan tracked the girls' progress as they disappeared through the side door. Bonnie's high-pitched giggles and Joy's playful words, soft and encouraging, sounded like ordinary neighborhood noises. Sweet noises found on Main Street, USA. And totally different from the clamor and dissonance he'd known as a kid. He pushed the memories away. After so many years, they didn't affect him anymore. Thankfully, little Bonnie would have a happy time with Joy.

He motioned to Jax and they both went inside. The evening stretched ahead of them. Especially him. Joy wouldn't be able to walk the beach later on, not with her responsibility for a child. His step slowed as the new reality hit. Three weeks ago, he would have cheered. Three weeks ago, he'd wanted her evicted. What the hell had happened to him?

After making quick work of a frozen dinner, Logan sat at his computer, organizing his photos—more than a hundred of them—into files by subject matter. And deleting the ones that didn't live up to standard. His standard. Every picture had to tell a story. To be so lifelike viewers would feel they could walk right in, down that sun-dappled road. Or wince at the acrid aroma of hot solder as a worker mended steel. When he pointed his camera, he aimed at the truth.

He wasn't Ansel Adams with landscapes. But he tried. He hadn't taken portraits of Eisenhower or Einstein like Yousuf Karsh, but he tried to capture the essence of his subjects in the same way. His subjects. Ordinary people. Everyday heroes.

One by one, he examined each shot. And discovered landscapes. Seascapes. Cityscapes. Cracked sidewalks, a firehouse, a child coming through a bakery door, his face covered in powdered sugar and his grin stretching from ear to ear. Logan chuckled. Oh, yeah. He definitely remembered taking that one. He moved on to several pictures of Adam Fielding at work with his patients. The vet was totally unconscious of his photographer's presence. Exactly what Logan hoped for.

If he waited long enough, if he had enough patience, the masks disappeared, uncovering the soul.

As Logan continued to examine his work, awareness started to bloom. He forgot to breathe as pictures of Joy filled the screen. Dozens of shots, each one of them worthy of keeping. Daytime, nighttime, on the beach, leaning over the porch, holding sea glass. He'd taken more photos of her than of all the others combined.

That fact shocked him, but he continued to look through those pictures, to search for...he didn't know exactly what, but something more elusive. And finally, staring right back at him, he found what he'd always hoped to reveal in others—the truth beneath the masks. He found that the soul displayed on the screen...was not only Joy's, but through her, his own.

And that truth scared the daylights out of him. He loved her.

##

"I don't know how single parents manage," said Joy. "I'm exhausted. And it's only been a few days."

Logan smiled. "It'll get easier, if you can get her to sleep through the night." He and Joy sat on the front porch Saturday morning, coffee in hand, watching Bonnie and Ajax play in the yard.

"I thought sleeping problems were reserved for infants," said Joy. "That's how much I know. But seeing her grandma yesterday helped. She seems more settled."

"She'll be fine, Joyful. Just fine. She's got you."

He loved the blush that rose to her cheeks. She was an easy read.

"Thanks." She glanced at her watch. "The stores await. Groceries, of course, and clothes for Bonnie. Marie gave me a check last week. She said she was delighted—and that's a quote—for Bonnie to have a real shopping partner."

Her gaze focused on the child. "For the first time, Logan, I'm worrying about Marie. She looked and sounded so…so…small yesterday at the hospital. Poor woman."

"She needs time. There's a lot of stubborn in her. But…you know you're dealing in some risky business here." Which was putting it mildly. Joy had a way of jumping in where angels feared to go. Marie needed more help than Joy could give.

She nodded. "I'm not leaving town, so I can always be the go-to person for Marie. And today it's shopping. Love it." Her eyes gleamed. She leaned closer and whispered, "It's all about the hunt!"

The what? What hunt? Which proved he knew nothing about women.

"What about the car seat?"

She flashed a grin. "Borrowed one. I asked around at school."

Figured. "Then the whole town knows Bonnie's here now."

"Of course. Why not? There are no secrets in Pilgrim Cove."

"Liar."

She ignored that comment and looked toward the street. He did, too, in time to see the local taxi pull up. "Expecting anyone?" he asked.

"No…"

But thirty seconds later, she ran toward the man who exited the cab. An older guy, fairly tall, his wavy brown hair sprinkled with gray. Joy's arms opened wide as did his. "Dad! Dad!" Logan watched the reunion with his full attention. They hugged, they rocked, her dad held her around the waist as they walked toward him, as if he hadn't seen her in years instead of a mere month.

He walked down the porch steps. So *this* was what family looked like. He found it hard to swallow. Only on television shows had he ever seen children so excited about a dad's appearance. He'd usually stayed out of the way when his foster fathers had come home. But as these two drew closer, he had to admit, they held nothing back. What he saw was real. Love. Tenderness. Joy. Well, some people were lucky.

"Logan! I want you to meet my dad, Maxwell MacKenzie. But everyone calls him Mac." The name rang a bell. Not many Maxwell MacKenzies running around. Logan extended his hand.

"He was in Boston…"

"I can speak for myself, butterfly." The man shook Logan's hand. "I hopped the ferry at Rowes Wharf on a whim. Wanted to get out of Beantown for a bit."

Wanted to check up on his daughter, more likely. "Glad to meet you."

The magpie took over, pointing to the house. "Logan lives downstairs, and I live upstairs. It's working out great."

Mac's eyebrows rose. He cocked his head toward his daughter. "Want to repeat that, Joyful? *What*, exactly, is working out great?"

Before she could reply, however, Bonnie ran to them, pausing when she saw Mac, but then skipped to Joy's side, Ajax at her heels. Mac smiled and seemed to relax. "Hello, little lady." He nodded toward Bonnie but turned again to Logan.

"Your daughter, then, Mr. Nash? A beautiful child."

Oh, boy. "I can't claim that honor." He glanced at his housemate. "Joyful?" he enunciated. "I'm guessing you and your dad haven't communicated lately?"

"Hmm…we've both been distracted." Glancing at her dad, she said, "Bonnie's staying with me for a while."

That gave the man pause, but not for long. "Oh, for crying out loud, honey. You're a glutton for punishment." He cocked his thumb toward Logan. "And what's his role in all this?"

Logan watched her eyes move between her dad and him. Saw her mouth tighten, saw the determined look on her face. Maybe overprotective fathers posed a challenge. She patted her dad's arm.

"Logan's a good guy. Come on upstairs, and I'll fill you in. You, too, Bonnie. Snack time. We'll go shopping later." She turned toward Mac. "How's the Central Park project going? Stainless steel, isn't it?"

"Bronze. Whimsy in bronze, but…hold on a minute. I'm not falling for your old tricks. No distractions."

Of course! Logan placed the name. MacKenzie, the sculptor. Contemporary public art. Chicago. New York. Miami. For the moment, Logan was sharing space with creative genius. The sculptor's work was in art industry magazines. Not to mention the *New York Times* magazine. Daisy Mac, too. And Joy had grown up with all this?

A vague memory came to him. Bart Quinn. *You'd fit right in with them.*

MacKenzie stepped back, looked from his daughter to Logan to Bonnie to the dog. Logan almost felt sorry for the guy. Joy must have run him ragged while growing up.

"What the hell is going on here?" Mac began loudly but lowered his voice when Bonnie startled. He stared at Joy. "You should know better than to play house. No man's worth your salt. It'll only hurt more later."

Joy's complexion paled to alabaster. Logan dashed over and held her, supported her. "Take it easy, magpie. Easy." But his blood raced; his body tensed. Nobody should treat Joy that way. And no one would.

"I don't know what secrets you have, MacKenzie, and I don't give a rat's ass about you being her father. You are not going to upset her like this. Not the woman who carries sunshine in her pocket wherever she goes. A woman who, with one smile, can light up the world. Don't you know your daughter deserves better than that?"

MacKenzie rocked back on his heels, his chin high, eyes bulging. Logan braced himself for a verbal assault. "Who are you to question me?" he asked, his tone low and gritty. "You know her for a month...you arrogant son of a... I'd give my life for her without thinking twice."

"Logan, Dad...please."

He barely heard her soft plea. Instead, he heard her father's question, who are you? Who. Are. You? And after thirty-four years, the answer was in his grasp. No more living in the background, no more shadow life. He wanted the sunshine.

"I'm the man who loves your daughter. And you'll have to live with that." Through it all, his arm had remained around her. He hadn't let go. Now he pulled her closer. "Joy?" he whispered, a familiar uncertainty rearing its head. He'd been too spontaneous, too fast. He'd probably scared her off. The one time...the most important time...and he hadn't thought everything through.

"Oh, yes." She hugged him tight. "We definitely have something going on here." She kissed him, her body relaxed and soft against his. Where she belonged.

The next time he glanced at Mac, the man was on the phone. "I'm calling your mother," he said to Joy.

"Oh, Dad...let's—"

"When you speak to her," interrupted Logan, "remind her that a month can be a long time. A soldier thinks it's an eternity. A distance runner can pace a thousand miles. And an ordinary guy, a skeptic like me...can learn to believe in miracles. A month, Mr. MacKenzie, can be a lifetime."

Both sets of eyes were on him. He'd always hated being front and center, but his discomfort didn't matter now. Silence stretched until Logan quietly asked, "How long did you need to figure out Joy's mom was the one?" And for the first time, Logan saw Mac at a loss. The man looked left, right, anywhere but at Logan.

Joy, on the other hand, clapped and shouted. "He's got you there, Dad." She peeped at Logan. "A minute!" she said. "As the story goes, he came, saw, and conquered in an entire minute. And then they trekked to a commune in Colorado like the couple of hippies they were. Or pretended to be."

Beautiful. Couldn't be better. "I'm thinking," he said with a grin, "that glass houses and stones don't go well together."

"I'm not done with you yet." Mac spoke into the phone. "Daisy! We have a situation. I don't know if she's still picking up strays, or she's met the love of her life. You better come down here."

"Oh, no!" Joy grabbed the cell. "Mom, I'm fine. I'm happy. Visit in a couple of weeks because I'm really busy right now." She kneeled in front of Bonnie, kissed her forehead. "And besides, my guest room's already taken."

CHAPTER TEN

Mac returned to Boston that evening, promising his next trip would include Daisy. Joy and Bonnie drove him to the ferry.

"Stop worrying, Dad. Logan's a wonderful person. Honorable. He would never have lasted with the military if he weren't."

"I'll be looking him up. You can be sure of that. You can't hide on the Internet."

"He's got nothing to hide."

"Everybody has their secrets, Joyful. The trick is to know if they're big ones or little ones."

Joy pulled up to the dock. Her dad got out but came to her window. "He says he loves you and you love him. Can I assume you've discussed your medical situation?"

"N-not yet. But we will."

Mac emitted a deep sigh. "If he's really the right one, you'll find your way. If he's not the right one, then he's not good enough for you."

But Logan was the one. Her Mr. Right. She loved him and…goodness, he'd fought for her—for her honor—against her own father. If that wasn't love, then…? "I love you, too, Dad."

He leaned in and kissed her cheek. "We'll be calling. Count on it."

"Bye, Mr. Mac," called Bonnie.

"So long, sweetie pie. See you next time."

Joy lingered, watching her father disappear on board. Her first love. She'd promised to marry him when she grew up. She and Glory argued about who would get him. "I'll marry you both," he'd say, carrying one in each arm.

Little girls needed so much that a dad could provide. She and Glory had been lucky. She checked out Bonnie in the rearview mirror. For the next month or so, this little girl would get her full attention.

Late the next afternoon, Joy dropped three bundles of new clothes on Bonnie's bed. Logan hadn't joined them on their excursion, but maybe that was for the best.

"Shopping? A mall?" He'd looked as though she'd offered him a case of measles when she'd invited him. "Err…hmm… No. I'll pass. But have a great time."

Now Joy sighed with satisfaction. "We did really well. Let's hang everything up so your pretty new clothes won't crease."

Bonnie immediately went to the bed and reached into a bag. "You can't leave stuff around." She pulled out an adorable pink dress with hearts embroidered around the neckline. "Can I wear this to school?"

"Of course. You can wear anything you want to school."

"This one, too?" She held up a red dress with three layers of ruffles around the hemline.

"Yes, yes. And the aqua pants outfit and the Minnie Mouse tunic and leggings, and the new tee shirts and jeans. Anything at all. It's fun to feel pretty."

The child's eyes shone. She ran to Joy and hugged her. "Am I pretty, Ms. Joy?"

"Oh, Bonnie, sweetheart. You're more than pretty. You're beautiful. Absolutely beautiful." Inside and out.

"Grandma says I'm pretty, but she can't know. She just loves me."

Smart, too. Was she only five? "Your grandma is a very wise lady. But now I have a great idea. Would you like to model your new wardrobe for Logan, like a fashion show?"

Childhood memories flashed. She and Glory, showing off new clothes for their dad, whether store-bought or handmade by Daisy. Mac made such a great audience. His daughters were the most beautiful and talented girls in the kingdom.

"Logan's not home," said Bonnie, reaching for another garment and stroking it. "He and Ajax weren't waiting for us like they always do."

Smart, pretty, and observant. "Always?"

"Yup. On the porch or in the backyard."

"Maybe he's out taking pictures again."

Bonnie cocked her head. "Oops, he's home now. I heard the door. It makes a groan-swish sound."

Joy heard nothing. "I think you're Supergirl with super good hearing. Thanks for telling me."

"Ooh, Ms. Joy. Maybe at our fashion show, Logan can take pictures. Last year in preschool, we had to dress up, and a man came and took pictures. Grandma bought mine."

Sounded like a class picture day. "You'll get a new one this year in kindergarten. And I'm sure Grandma will buy that one, too."

From exuberant to pensive in a nanosecond. "But she won't be able to see it very good…er, I mean, well." She climbed onto Joy's lap. "If Logan takes a picture now, we can bring it to the hospital."

Joy's arms closed around the child. Precious. Precious girl. "That's a great idea. Absolutely. I'll call him and ask."

No five-year-old should have to worry like Bonnie did. She wore the responsibility she felt toward Marie like a sweater on a cool day. Except every day was cool, and the weight of that sweater had became normal.

The fashion show took place in Logan's larger apartment, which sported a real living room where Bonnie could parade and twirl and, in general, show off. The man clapped and cheered with every outfit the child wore, yet managing to work his camera at the same time. Between helping Bonnie change clothes, then running to the sofa to sit next to Logan as part of the audience, Joy barely had time to thank him. And when she did, he brushed it away.

"Glad to do it. She's got a tough road ahead. Let her enjoy today. Let her enjoy being a little girl."

"That's exactly right," said Joy slowly. "A month of happy memories. And, of course, she'll still have me at school."

Bonnie came over, hugged Jax, then climbed onto the couch next to Logan and yawned. "When are the pictures going to be ready?"

"When you come home from school tomorrow. Looks like being a model is hard work. Or else, Joy tired you out today."

"Nope. I love shopping with Ms. Joy. But…I think I'm hungry."

"Oh, shoot. I forgot about dinner." Joy jumped to her feet and headed for the door. "How about hot dogs and beans?"

"Better yet, how about we go to the Lobster Pot?" asked Logan, just as Bonnie yawned again. "Or we can save that for another time. Hot dogs sound just right."

"But I love the Lobster Pot…" For the first time, a whining note crept into Bonnie's voice.

"We can't have you falling asleep in your soup, can we?" Logan teased. "Not very ladylike."

Joy listened to the little exchange, impressed. He really was good at distracting her. "Let's get you changed into your new pj's, eat dinner, and have a story. How's that for a great way to end the day?"

"And school's tomorrow," Bonnie added. "Goody. Can you use one of Logan's new pictures on the bulletin board when I'm Star of the Day?"

"You bet."

Bonnie raced to her mentor and hugged tight. "I love you, Ms. Joy."

"And I love you, too, Bon-Bon."

She happened to glance at Logan and saw his forehead wrinkle before he leaned back and closed his eyes.

She knew what he was thinking. He wasn't alone in his concerns.

An hour later, Bonnie was fast asleep, and Joy's kitchen was spotless. "Wow. Thanks. I appreciate the help."

Logan shrugged. "What's a few minutes? You're sort of working two jobs now."

In a way, he was right. She'd never been busier or more tired or scattered. She'd even started making lists.

"If you weren't her teacher for the rest of the year," said Logan, "I'd be waving caution lights in your face."

No small talk here. "I know."

"Her stay here will end. And then what?"

"And then she'll be with Marie. I'll miss her—a-a lot—but I want Bonnie to be happy."

He gathered her into his arms. "I should have realized her happiness would be your priority. You always want the best for everyone."

A butterfly kiss landed on her forehead; a trail of them followed down her cheek until his mouth reached hers. Everything and everyone else vanished. There was only Logan.

The fragrance of his aftershave—cool, spicy, like the outdoors—made her inhale more deeply. It was so right for him. She ran her tongue along his lips, then inside his mouth. His kiss morphed from gentle to urgent in an instant.

"You make me feel like a teenager," he whispered, "on his first date."

His embrace tightened, and they were so tightly woven together she felt his hunger, the same hunger that skimmed down her own body from head to toe. Joy's senses reeled, her heart rate zoomed, powered by an electricity reserved for love. She tightened her hold on him as her legs trembled. But when his hand cupped her breast, stroked it gently across the nipple, her knees gave way.

"Joy?" His voice was hoarse. "It's your call. Now or stop."

"Now. Definitely now."

"Oh, sweetheart…"

"Just let's check on Bonnie first and make sure she's sleeping."

Ten steps to the child's door. Jax lay on the oval carpet at the side of the bed. His tail wagged, but he remained in place. Bonnie slept, her breaths light and even.

"'Atta girl," whispered Logan.

Joy turned in his arms, bestowed a kiss on his mouth. In lockstep, they walked to her bedroom and paused on the threshold. Moonlight shone through the window. "No lamps needed," whispered Joy.

"Very romantic, but I'd know you in the dark," he said, pulling the bedspread down with one hand and easing her onto the bed with the other. He leaned over her, his mouth touching hers, his kisses exploratory, then urgent. And she met that urgency with an identical yearning. Somehow clothing disappeared, a shirt on the bed, slacks on the floor, every garment this way and that.

Finally skin to skin, his hard body and her softer one, wrapped round each other like pieces in a puzzle. A perfect fit.

His hand skimmed across her breasts. She gasped and her legs tightened around his, her core muscles tightening inside, too. Breathing seemed optional. She didn't know, didn't care. Until she had to drag air into her lungs. She kissed his neck, his mouth, stroked his back and shoulders. She wanted to surround him the way he was surrounding her.

Logan loved her reaction to him. No games, no hesitations, no coyness. With his every stroke, he made her shiver. His palm cupped her breasts and traveled lower, stroking her thighs, closer and closer and finally skimming the most sensitive part of her. She arched her back and groaned. He touched her inside. She was already moist.

"Oh, oh…"

"You are as wet and ready as you're going to be," he whispered, reaching for his slacks on the floor.

She heard a crackle of paper before Logan raised himself over her. He didn't need the protection, but she said nothing, just smiled and opened her arms to welcome him, a moment later pleased that he'd entered slowly and carefully. And then it didn't matter.

Like a match to dry kindling, she ignited. Banked fires burst into flame. He wasn't her first, but the past was irrelevant. She'd never loved another man like this, never felt as passionate as this. She absorbed him— sexually, visually, lovingly. A new chapter was beginning for her. If only…

Again all thought vanished as she traveled faster and faster with Logan to that tempting, all-consuming goal. A riot of color, the hot reds and oranges filled her mind. Until every muscle quivered, and she shattered into a million fragile pieces.

Logan was certainly no virgin, but he'd never before made love to a woman so precious. So precious to him that he wanted to stay forever. Joy, Joy, Joy. His joy. His new beginning. A month ago, he'd thought she was a dizzy, immature girl. He'd been so wrong. Now he trusted her. A woman with a soft heart, a big heart. A loving heart. The wonder of it, to his amazement and delight, was that she'd offered that love to him. They sure did "have something going here."

His disappointments from the past faded. Childhood was over. He wasn't alone anymore. He trusted her. He'd trust in a forever.

The visit to the apple orchard the following weekend had been a last-minute plan put together by Logan and Adam. A gorgeous autumn day couldn't go to waste. Joy wholeheartedly approved. She, Rebecca, Bonnie, Sara, and her best friend, Katie, climbed into Adam's van. Bonnie sat in her car seat next to the "big" girls, her eyes as big as saucers and her smile as wide as a jack-o'-lantern's.

"All aboard!" called out Adam from behind the wheel.

Bonnie giggled. Sara groaned. "Dad, it's not a train!" She turned her head to face the last row of seats. "Mom, tell him."

But Rebecca was chuckling. "He's just having fun. And we all can use some fun. If he wants a train, then we'll be a train. Choo-choo." Her imitation echoed, and instantly, three little girls followed suit.

"You and Sara are quite remarkable," said Joy, studying the easy interaction between Rebecca and her new daughter. "It's like you've known each other forever, and yet, you and Adam are newlyweds yourselves."

"I guess I was very lucky," said Rebecca. "I fell in love with Adam, and, well…Sara is very easy to love. And she so much needed…no, change that to *wanted*. She so much wanted a mom." She shifted in her seat to face Joy. "She was about five when her mother died, so she definitely has some memories. Good ones, too. But are vague memories enough to help her grow up? Despite Adam's devotion, figuring out womanhood can be kind of complicated. Don't you think?"

"Oh, yeah." Her friend couldn't realize how accurately she'd summed up Joy's situation. *Complicated* merely scratched the surface. Joy kept the subject on the children.

"I don't know what Bonnie knows or remembers about her parents, but she never speaks of a mother or father. Thank God for Marie."

Rebecca's glance held a wealth of meaning. "Learning to use a prosthesis was very hard work. Months of therapy. Physical and emotional. And I'm only thirty. So I say, thank God for you, for giving Marie an R and R."

Joy shrugged. "I don't mind. I love kids. And as you said about Sara, my Bon-bon is very easy to love. I'll help Marie out when she comes home."

"Good of you…but…" Rebecca remained silent as they turned off the highway onto a narrow country road. Signs for the orchard became visible, and the conversation turned to safety rules while climbing trees.

"Can we practice having head counts?" asked Joy after they'd all exited the vehicle. "That's what I do with my class."

"Looks to me like we have three beautiful princesses plus four bossy adults. How many is that?" posed Adam.

"Seven." Bonnie spoke first. "We did the number seven in school."

"You must have a great teacher," said Logan with a gleam in his eye.

"Oh, I do. I do. Ms. Joy is the best!"

Logan squatted in front of Bonnie. "Want to know a secret?" he whispered.

Her mouth rounded into a perfect O. "What?"

"I think she's the best, too."

Sara and Katie giggled. Adam's eyebrow rose, and Rebecca smiled. Joy's face burned. "For crying out loud…Logan! C'mon, it's time to pick some apples and arrange for the class trip next week."

"Yes, teacher."

Rebecca elbowed her husband. "He's got a bad case."

"Just like I do." He wrapped his arm around her. "I can hardly recognize him as the same guy who first came into the office. What a difference a woman makes."

"The right woman."

The gentle teasing flowed around Joy. But her friend's statement nagged at her. The right woman. Was she the right one for Logan? She watched him play with Bonnie, gently teasing but protective, too. So natural. With his dark memories of childhood, he may not have realized what a blessing children were until now. There was no going back. Yes, he loved her. She loved him. But until Logan knew and understood her limitations, the question of being the right woman would remain unanswered. He'd never become a dad if he stayed with her. She couldn't wait much longer to tell him.

##

Logan leaned over the railing of the commuter ferry heading to Boston. He didn't want to screw up. When he asked Joy to marry him, he wanted everything to be perfect. Like in the classic movies. A beautiful setting— maybe Boston Gardens on a gentle Sunday morning, or maybe on the beach at sunset, or maybe he'd rent a boat from the marina. He wasn't sure of where, but it had to be romantic.

And the ring… It had to be a sparkling diamond ring. Not too small but not too big, either. Heck. He couldn't afford gaudy. But his finances were in pretty good shape—not much to spend on in war zones. Hmm…maybe he should visit his accountant in person and collect the statements that had accumulated. Of course, he saw them online, but maybe a personal visit was in order. Or maybe he just wanted to share his happiness with someone not living in Pilgrim Cove!

He'd never dreamed he would be lucky enough to enjoy the extraordinary life of an ordinary man. A husband. And someday, a father. He never dreamed he'd find a person with whom he could share his past and look forward to the future. Just like all couples do.

Joy was incredible. He trusted her. He loved her. She loved him. That's what mattered. The city's skyline came into view. In his pocket was a folded paper with the names and addresses of three jewelry stores. He took it out, unfolded it, and scratched his head.

"Holy Toledo," he mumbled. "I'm on the hunt!"

CHAPTER ELEVEN

"I want Grandma."

Uh-oh. The plaintive note in Bonnie's voice signaled a meltdown on the way. The school day was over. Rain had fallen nonstop since morning, the dreariness probably adding to Bonnie's cranky mood.

"Of course you want to see Grandma." Joy opened her arms. "Come cuddle before I make supper, and we'll plan a visit."

The child climbed onto Joy's lap without hesitation and leaned her whole weight against her.

"Tired, Bon-Bon?"

"I w-want to see Grandma."

It seemed like Bonnie's mind was one-track. "We can visit tomorrow after school. How about if we take her some of the apples you picked?"

"Yes! A present that she can touch."

"And smell."

Bonnie leaned outward, better to see Joy. "That's right. Smell, too. She can touch and smell and hear and taste. But she can't see." Bonnie released a sob and a sigh, the combination so mournful that Joy wanted to cry.

"She can still hug and kiss you. We'll go tomorrow after school." Joy pulled the girl against her again and kissed her head and cheek. She rocked her. "You are the best five-year-old in the whole world, Bon-Bon. But don't tell the other kids in class, okay?"

Bonnie perked up. "Another secret? I won't tell." She jumped from Joy's lap and went to Happy's open cage. "Want to take a walk, Happy?" The bird hopped from the cage doorway to Bonnie's shoulder, gaily chirping her own songs.

Joy would have joined in…if she could carry a tune. Tears avoided, and Bonnie seemed happy again. The child had adjusted so well to her temporary life with Joy that any crying took Joy by surprise. Bonnie was quite remarkable. Marie had done a fine job.

"Grandma's room is the next one on the right," said Joy. Bonnie skipped ahead, carrying a basket of ripe, delicious apples.

The hospital was twenty miles from Pilgrim Cove; darkness was falling fast. Joy yawned. Maybe they'd stop at a fast-food joint for a quick supper. Not for the first time, she wondered how single parents managed everything. Her teaching position required her full attention, but so did Bonnie. She did, however, fall asleep almost instantly these days.

She entered Marie's room after Bonnie. The girl was already chatting nonstop about her visit to the orchard and had put an apple in her grandmother's hand. Joy's greater attention, however, was paid to Marie, noting the woman's combed hair and lipstick. But also noting her pallor and weight loss. Her right arm was in a full-length cast—for a broken wrist? But her leg—oh, her poor right leg was in a full cast, too.

But the woman smiled; her eyes twinkled. "Guess what, Joy? I have good news."

"It must be wonderful news."

"I'm being transferred to rehab tomorrow. Back to Pilgrim Cove. Yay!"

"Fantastic. You've made great progress."

"With my left hand for sure." Marie grinned, and Joy saw the real woman emerge. "I've got a social worker assigned to me, and she arranged it. Being back in town will be easier for all of us, and my other friends, especially for visiting."

Bonnie jumped up and down. Then looked at Joy. "What's rehab?"

"It's where Grandma will learn to get stronger by doing exercises. And then one day when the casts are removed, she'll be able to walk and do everything again as usual."

"Good." said Bonnie. "Everything as usual...except"—she looked up at Joy—"do you want to live with us?"

##

"And that's when my heart broke," said Joy, recounting her visit to the hospital to Logan. They were on the deck of the Crow's Nest the next evening, sitting next to each other in lounge chairs. Bonnie was sound asleep in her bedroom with Jax snoozing in her doorway. Everyone where they belonged, at least on that night.

The rain had gone. Clear skies hosted a bright crescent moon, looking like an ornament in the night sky. A cool evening but not too chilly, autumn was showing off the best of her wares. Joy wore one of her crocheted ponchos, perfect for such weather.

Logan reached for her hand, his fingers intertwining with hers. "Temporary families are tough. Some hearts break; others harden. What did Marie say?"

"Nothing much. Just looked at me and told Bonnie that I'd visit them often, to which I agreed." She shrugged. "What else could she say?"

"Maybe that social worker will figure something out for her. Not that I have much belief in social workers."

She squeezed his hand. "From what you've told me, I can't blame you."

She couldn't imagine adjusting to so many families during the course of a childhood. Foster parents had different motivations. Sometimes he'd gotten lucky, but most times not.

He leaned over and stole a kiss. "While Marie was relating her good news, I had some, too, and the timing couldn't be better."

Her curiosity ignited. "Tell me," she ordered.

"*Nat Geo* wants me to do another series on the canine-human connection. Starting with therapy dogs and service dogs." He leaned in. "There is a difference, you know."

"I'm sure I'll learn about it after the stories are written." She raised her head and kissed him. "Congratulations. You must feel proud. It's such a quality magazine, and if they do a television show…?"

"I countered the offer."

His casual manner made her sit up straight. Either he was foolish or totally secure in his work. "That took guts. Was it about money?"

"Nah, the money's all right. I wanted to include other service animals like miniature horses, monkeys, and parrots." He looked toward the Atlantic. "When I take an assignment, I like to go deep and wide in the research, but more important, I want to bring the reader into the story in my own way."

"You sound just like my folks. Artistic temperament."

"More like artistic freedom. Words and pictures. My own research, my own interviews and personal visits. The more info I have, the better decisions I can make." He seemed to hesitate. "That's how it works, Joy. I've got to do the whole thing and make it my own."

He didn't have to over-explain. She'd grown up surrounded by creative personalities with vision. "I get it, Logan. It's a creative process. But you still haven't told me the end of the story. What did the magazine say about your requests?"

He grinned. "Maybe I shouldn't have chanced it, now that there are two of us. But would I be telling you all this if negotiations had bombed?"

The *two of us* part sounded wonderful. "Well, of course you would. At least, I hope so. That's wh-what people who are in relationships do. They share—good news or bad. No need to keep the disappointments hidden. No need to keep secrets. Not anymore," she added softly.

Tell him. This is a good time to tell him.

His loving expression, a yearning look, so open, so readable. She wondered if he saw it reflected on her face. "You are so incredible. How did I get so lucky?"

He jumped from his chaise, pushed it aside, and sat next to her. His hands cupped her face. "I love you. I love saying it. I love your name. It suits you so perfectly. You are a joy. And you're joyful. Your parents gave birth to a winner."

His kisses proved his words. She wound her arms around his neck, took him close to her heart. "I love you, too, Logan." She couldn't remember if she'd spoken those three little words aloud before, or if they'd remained quiet thoughts in her mind.

"I hope you're still saying that in fifty years," said Logan, "because I'm in for the long haul."

Oh, he was going fast, but so was her heartbeat. "What…what…"

"I'm probably messing up. I wanted to choose the most romantic setting and sweep you off your feet, but I think you swept me off mine." He kneeled on the deck and took both her hands in his. "Joyful MacKenzie, I love you with all my heart. Will you marry me?"

Yes! But it was too late. Too late. She'd just thrown away the rest of her life.

No smile, no laughter. No delight. Logan froze. How could he have misread her? She loved him. Hell, she'd fought with her father because of him. He saw her eyes close and heard her rapid breathing.

"Logan. Logan. I can't say yes right now…b-because I have to tell you something. To be fair to you." Tears welled and ran down her cheeks.

The tears threw him. His hands tightened on hers. "What's wrong? Tell me. I'll help you. Whatever it is. Are you sick? We'll make it better." Could there be someone else? His mind raced to their night together. No. She'd been free and loving, but now fear threatened to clog his throat.

"I-I'm not exactly sick, but you probably want kids, and we should have discussed this earlier, but we were so busy, and I was afraid to admit it, but you have to know that…I-I can't have children. And I'm so sorry."

Her sobs killed him. Deep, soul-wrenching sobs. So unlike the girl he knew. The sunshine girl.

"Please stop crying, Joy. Please. You're tearing me up. I've never thought about kids. It doesn't matter to me." He could tell she was listening but still hadn't raised her head. He plunged on. "Heck, there are so many unwanted children everywhere...I've seen them." He took her in his arms and whispered, "I was an unwanted child myself, and the world doesn't need more kids."

He felt her arms slide around him, her light weight resting against him.

"You're so good with Bonnie," she said. "A natural. You'd be a wonderful father. But with me...you'll never have the chance. That's so unfair."

The irony was not lost on him. The teacher with the big heart couldn't have children of her own. "Unfair to you more than me. I'm not ready for kids. I never thought about having children, about being a father. Remember, I wasn't even sure I could handle Ajax. And I never dreamed I'd be lucky enough to meet you."

A tiny smile emerged, encouraging him to press on.

"And if one day, we decide we want a family, we can follow Brad and Angie's lead, right? Adopt a few."

"Really?"

"Really. But that's in the future. Right now, let's just be a couple. I'm looking forward to sharing life just with you."

"My ovaries...I don't have them anymore."

"Bad, nasty things. Better to get rid of them."

She stroked his cheek, the palm of her hand warm. "Yes. But I don't have any surprises in a lab. No saved eggs or anything. So this is for real, Logan. You have to know that."

Her words were serious, but hope dawned in her eyes. A smile teased the corners of her mouth. He smiled back.

"And this is also your last chance to back out," she added.

"Are you kidding? It took me thirty-four years to find you!" He reached into his front pocket and took out the ring. "I'm going to do this one more time," he said. "And you'd better give me the right answer."

She didn't wait. "Yes, yes, and yes." She extended her arm, and he slipped the ring on her fourth finger, hoping he hadn't made a mistake in his choice.

"It's beautiful," she whispered.

"I wasn't sure," he said "So many rings looked alike. When I spotted this one, the sapphire reminded me of your eyes...and the little diamonds were their sparkle. But we can change it. I want you to be happy."

"I am happy. No change required. It's beautiful, and so are you. In fact, you did everything right. Sea View House is a romantic setting. Look out there. Moon, stars, and the ocean at our doorstep. It's magic, and it doesn't get better than this."

Maybe she had a point. Seemed that all the planning in the world couldn't stave off surprises.

"My mom was correct again."

"Oh?"

"She said that when I met the right man, he would love me for myself. And if he didn't, he wasn't the right man."

"Smart mom."

"Mind if I call her? It's not every day a daughter receives a marriage proposal."

He loved that he was part of that special couple. "Go for it. But do me a favor...wait a while before inviting them down. Your dad needs time to decompress. And I'd like time to be alone...just us." He wanted to savor their relationship, get used to being part of a pair. Finally, he had someone he could count on. Someone he could trust. Cozy and solid. He'd never had that pleasure before and looked forward to enjoying every moment.

"Alone? Just us?" she questioned. "Have you forgotten about Bonnie?"

Oops. "Guilty as charged. My thoughts are all about you. I guess I'll survive another couple of weeks until she's back with Marie and things are normal here again." He kissed her and had a terrific idea. "After Bonnie leaves, how'd you like to move into the Captain's Quarters?"

"After Bonnie leaves, I'm hoping Bart will come up with a more permanent option for both of us."

"Then I'll take that as a yes."

CHAPTER TWELVE

Joy stuck by Logan's side, and Bonnie stuck by Joy's side—for the first five minutes of the invasion on Saturday. That was the way Logan looked at the MacKenzie family visit. His new fiancée called it a family party. Logan doubted she had a clue as to how overwhelming the MacKenzies could be all at once.

They'd shown up quickly, one after the other, and now filled Sea View House—upstairs, downstairs, every nook and cranny. If he once thought her mom would wait awhile before coming to see her newly engaged daughter, he'd learned differently. And if Daisy came, then Mac came. Joy's brother, Chance, had to check out the guy who'd captured his little sister—bringing his wife, Anabel, and their two little boys with them. Even the elusive Glory had shown up and could stay for a few hours before getting back to the theater.

But now he and Joy were alone in his kitchen, putting out paper plates and utensils for lunch.

"I'm really glad they're all here," said Joy. "I want to show you off."

"I'm not used to…"

She squeezed his arm. "I know, but you're doing great. Just like Bonnie. Look how she's taken charge of my nephews." She grinned up at him. "You have to admit, Ajax is such a cool icebreaker."

"And Bonnie's a cool kid. With all the practice she's had, she can handle just about anything."

"So can you." She stood on tiptoe and kissed him on the cheek. "Not going to run away from this horde, are you?"

Catching her around the waist, he pulled her close. "Never. I love you, but I'm glad your family's not staying for a week!" They walked back to the main part of his apartment. His glance swept across the living room, pausing a moment at each person there.

"Mac had the picture I sent framed. Your mother told me. She loved it, too."

"It must have been something special."

He shrugged. "I don't know which one he chose. I sent a dozen." A bubble of laughter rose from Joy, and he hugged her again. "But my plan worked. I won him over."

"Did you say a dozen? I can't remember any photo sessions...."

He felt his mouth turn up. "You should know better than that by now."

Her brow furrowed, and she bit her bottom lip. A moment later, she looked at him with delight. "Oh, of course. You're serious about every shot you take. Each time you pick up your camera is a photo session."

"Bingo. I was...let's say, curious, about your dad's reaction. If none of the pictures meant anything, then..." He shrugged again, trying to appear nonchalant when, at the time he'd mailed the package, his nerve endings had been raw. He'd wanted Mac to come around. He'd wanted Mac's approval, the idea of which made his stomach knot again. Winning approval was a child's game he'd always lost. And didn't play as an adult. He didn't need anyone's approval except for professional editors in regard to his work. And if he were good enough with his camera and ideas, the work could speak for itself.

"You don't have to spare my feelings," said Joy. "I know my dad can be stubborn and overprotective with his kids. But, Logan, we're in this together now. So you can share your hopes and fears with me."

"I guess I haven't gotten used to that part yet."

"The real question is, can you get used to them?" She waved at the crowd. "You just got yourself a family. They're noisy, opinionated, *always* know what's best for you…but they'll always have your back."

That was an idea he'd never explored…never had the need. "I'm sure you're right about all that," he said, "but…I also know for sure that if we don't feed them, they'll disappear fast enough."

She slapped him lightly on the shoulder. "The Lobster Pot van should be pulling up soon."

On cue, the doorbell rang and a familiar voice called out, "Special delivery. Come and get it."

"Bart Quinn!" said Joy, racing to the front of the house. "Why is he delivering food instead of listing homes?"

Logan tugged the door open, saw Joy take one look at Bart and the attractive woman next to him before yelling, "Auntie Honey! Come in, come in. How did you get here?" She kissed "Auntie Honey" and turned around. "This is my mom's sister."

Daisy came flying over.

"Mom," said Joy, "did you know Auntie Honey was coming?"

"Looks like Auntie Honey's staying," Logan whispered, nodding at the woman's suitcase. He wondered how many more family surprises there could be.

"Someone forgot to pick up this beautiful lady at the pier," said Bart, his bright blue eyes making the rounds. "Now, Joyful, I'm not saying who the culprit was…but how could anyone forget about Honeybelle, such a delightful woman who knows how to tell a good story?"

"That's a first," whispered Joy. "She told him her real name."

"Joy's innocent here," said Daisy, hugging her sister. "I'm so sorry, Honey. I just lost track of time."

"Seems to run in the family," said Bart, with a wink at Joy, "just like the high spirits."

"All's well that ends well," said the new arrival, "and Mr. Quinn here came to my rescue. Nice to know that knights in shining armor still exist."

The woman commanded center stage. Tall, arrow-straight posture, and if her beauty was starting to fade, it didn't matter. The woman was vibrant. Knew how to play her audience. No question where Glory had inherited her talent and presence.

Logan gestured toward Bart and whispered to Joy, "Get a look at his face. He's—he's smitten."

"Great vocabulary. You nailed it."

The illustrious Bartholomew Quinn was actually blushing; his bright blue eyes, now focused on Honey, were more luminous than the sun.

"Come on, everyone," Logan said. "Grab a box from the car, and let's eat." He looked toward his landlord. "There's enough for you, too, Bart. Want to join us?"

"Don't mind if I do. In fact, there's an ice-cold six-pack out there I tucked in…just in case, ya know?"

"Yeah," he sighed. "I know."

"Now do you believe in the magic of the place?" asked Bart, pointing a finger at Logan and gesturing at the crowd. "Not alone anymore, are ya?"

"No comment."

##

Joy hovered near the children in the corner of the living room, making herself appear busy but eavesdropping on their conversation. Ajax sat with them. Sooner or later, Joy knew she'd be laughing.

"You are so lucky to have Ajax." The voice came from five-year-old Dillon.

"I love Jax." Bonnie hugged the dog and received a lick for her efforts. "He loves me, too." She looked at her two new playmates, Dillon and little Conner. "Ajax is like my brother."

Joy hid a smile, but the boys nodded in agreement. "Maybe Mom and Dad could get us that kind of brother," said Dillon. "He'd be better than a regular one."

Joy suppressed a giggle. Worth the effort of hiding in plain sight, but she'd have to warn her sister-in-law, Anabel.

"Living with Auntie Joy must be fun," said Dillon.

Bonnie beamed. "It's so nice. I love Jax, but I love Ms. Joy more. She's like my auntie, too."

"Or your mom."

Whoops. This was dangerous territory for Bonnie. Their living arrangement wasn't forever. Joy listened closely, prepared to intervene.

"I don't have a mom anymore, but I have a grandma, and she's in the hospital." Tears started to run down her face, and Joy took a step closer.

Little Connor began to pat Bonnie's leg. "Don't cry, don't cry."

Joy swept to the floor and hauled Bonnie onto her lap. "Grandma's getting better, remember? And we'll visit her tomorrow—right here in Pilgrim Cove at the rehab center. Isn't that great?"

Bonnie nodded against Joy's chest and clung to her.

"How about we all take this big, furry guy for a walk on the beach? We've been inside long enough."

"Yes, yes." The boys scrambled up from the floor. "See, Bonnie? Auntie Joy always has the best ideas."

"I know that," Bonnie agreed slowly. "Jax loves the beach, and so do I."

"And I love all you guys." Joy gave them each a kiss, which Dillon promptly wiped away. She hugged Bonnie again.

Within five minutes, the house emptied, except for Bart and Honey, and the party moved outdoors. Surrounded by the three children and Jax, Joy led the way, still thinking about Bonnie. Her spirit was heavier than she would have liked.

Soon the pack of humans began to drift and separate into smaller groups. To Joy's astonishment, Ajax showed another side of himself. "What's he doing?"

"I guess you can't fight DNA," said Logan. "He's minding his flock."

Jax chased after Dillon and herded him back from the waterline. He ran to Connor when the child fell down and waited with him until he was on his feet again. Then urged him toward the others. The dog ran in front of the group—adults and kids—and then to the back, keeping them together and never stopping in his mission.

"He's worth every penny you must have spent for him," said Anabel. "Where can I get one?"

"Ajax is a long story," said Logan. "But there's a way you can apply for a retired MWD."

"The boys will be over the moon," said Joy. "But I'm surprised at your question. You and Chance have never spoken about getting a dog before."

"Never really thought about it, but a dog like Ajax can be another set of eyes and ears." Anabel patted her stomach and stared at Joy with worried eyes. "I don't like secrets so I'm going to tell you now. Chance and I…we've got a third one on the way."

A surprise Joy wasn't prepared for. She felt Logan's arm tighten around her, his mouth near her ear. "You okay?"

"Of course," she said, pasting a smile on her face while a wave of grief passed through her. She just needed more time. She stepped to Anabel and embraced her. "Congratulations, Mama. You and Chance must be excited. Why didn't you say something earlier?"

"Are you kidding? Today was about you and Logan…especially Logan. Your folks would have disowned me for stealing the spotlight." Anabel walked toward the man in question. "Speaking as the one other in-law in this crowd, welcome to this crazy family. And please, please make her happy."

##

Daisy's hug at the end of the day left Joy breathless. "Next time, bring Logan home to P-town. We think you picked a winner. Now pick a date for the wedding."

"We'll let you know. Think small, Mom. Small. Maybe Christmas?"

"Two months? Whew, but we'll do it." She embraced Joy again. "Your Logan is crazy about you, and he's so good with little Bonnie."

"I'm glad you and Dad feel that way. Chance, too." Her brother had cornered her awhile ago to give her a thumbs-up. Now her breath hitched. "It would have been terrible if Dad and Logan—"

"Oh, please. As soon as Dad saw those beautiful pictures… Your Logan is a clever man."

Joy beamed. "Talented as well." She told her about *Nat Geo*. "The only downside is the traveling. But I suppose I'll get used to it."

"You can't hold him back, honey. Wonderful offers don't come around every day. But your own career should keep you busy. You love it, so never give it up."

"No fear of that." She glanced over her shoulder. "Mom…what am I doing with Auntie Honey?"

Daisy rolled her eyes. "Well, she's got a flight to Florida on Monday. Just get her to the local ferry, and she'll get herself to the airport. She's determined to buy a condo down south. No more New England winters for her."

"Is she retiring? Closing the gallery?" Joy couldn't envision her active aunt as a lady of leisure.

"I have no idea. Honey has a way of revealing herself *after* she does something."

Joy's thoughts raced ahead. "I suppose Bonnie can sleep with me, and Auntie can use Bonnie's room."

"Already taken care of. Logan preempted that lovely Mr. Quinn from offering her accommodation. Auntie Honey is staying right here in Logan's guest room." She rubbed the back of her neck and emitted a deep sigh. "But it seems your Realtor is taking her on a tour of Pilgrim Cove tomorrow. And then out to dinner."

"Oh, my God. I love Auntie Honey, but this man has really been good to me. She'd better not—"

Daisy raised her brows. Her hand came up in a stop motion. "Mr. Quinn's old enough to look out for himself."

She had a point, but… "The way it works around here, Mom, is that Bart Quinn always looks out for everyone else."

"And don't you do the same?" She waved toward Bonnie. "You've stepped in where only angels dare to go. She's a darling girl, Joy, and she adores you. She also needs you. But you're starting a new life with Logan, and you don't need complications."

Bon-Bon, however, already owned her heart. "Don't be concerned about her or me. She's mine only for another couple of weeks. She has a devoted grandma who loves her completely."

"I understand, Joy. I also understand that sometimes people do extraordinary things in the name of love."

##

Bonnie ran ahead of Joy as soon as she spotted her grandmother in the community room of the rehab center. Marie was in a wheelchair, her right leg still in a cast and propped up. Her hair was pulled back with a pink ribbon, and she wore matching lipstick. Despite her efforts, Joy thought she looked pale and exhausted, but she perked up as soon as she heard Bonnie.

"Hugs, hugs, my Bonnie-belle."

"But gently," cautioned Joy. "Grandma's still getting better."

"Let's rub noses like Eskimos," said Marie.

Bonnie giggled and complied. "Ms. Joy calls me Bon-Bon. We brought you chocolate bars today and more of your favorite apples. Delicious!" She glanced at Joy. "It's a word joke 'cause it tastes delicious and the name is Delicious. Isn't that funny?"

"Very funny." But the most delicious part of the visit was seeing Marie smile. Joy kept half an ear on the conversation while looking around the facility. One thing was certain. Marie was not alone. Assistance was a button call away.

"Hi, Marie, I'm sitting right next to you, on the good left side."

"I'm glad to be back home," said Marie, turning her head toward Joy. "Or almost home. But I'm afraid it's going to take awhile longer. At my age, bones don't knit as fast as they used to." She sighed. "Bonnie sounds wonderful. But how are you managing? Are you okay?"

"More than okay. I have—"

"Good, good." She called for Bonnie. "Sweetie, would you share your apples with my friends here in this room? Say your grandma has plenty to go around."

Bonnie glanced at Joy, uncertain. "Go ahead, Bon-Bon. I'll be right here. I think they'll like meeting you. And they'll like the apples."

"Cause they're delicious!" Seemed she loved her joke.

"Is she gone?" asked Marie. "I need to speak to you alone."

"What's going on?"

"Remember that social worker on my case? Now she's asking a lot of questions about later. What are my plans for when I get out of here? What arrangements have been made? Who's going to take care of me at discharge? All that stuff."

"Does she know about Bonnie?"

Marie smiled. "Yes. She's the same woman I first saw at the hospital. When I met her there, we chatted like friends. She made the arrangements for me to come here, which I appreciated. But I didn't realize that what I told her could be used against me. Fortunately, I told her Bonnie was living with her guardian."

"Which is the truth. Did she back off?"

"For now, but…" Her breath came out on a sob. She held crumpled tissues in her hand, which she raised to her mouth, her eyes. "I can't hide it anymore. From myself, I mean. The real truth is, I don't know how I can continue to raise a lively youngster. I-I can barely take care of myself."

Joy bit back her own tears as she stroked the older woman's hand. "But you're not your rip-roaring usual Marie right now because you're under the weather. You'll feel differently when you're back on your feet."

Marie stayed quiet for a moment before replying. "Maybe. But I need an insurance policy. Something more than the housekeeper I told the social worker I'd hire when I got home."

"A housekeeper's not a bad idea."

"Not a great one, either. Cleaning and cooking is fine. But raising Bonnie?" She let the question linger.

Her hints couldn't be more obvious. Joy reached for Marie's hand and guided the woman's fingers to the ring Logan had given her.

"I have some wonderful news," said Joy.

Marie touched the ring all around.

"It's a sapphire nested in tiny diamonds."

"Sounds beautiful. Is it from Logan?"

"Yes. Yes, it's Logan. And we're very happy."

Marie opened her arms to embrace Joy. "I liked him, too. And Bonnie talks about him a lot. Logan and his dog. We should celebrate. It looks like everything will work out for everyone. Simply perfect!"

Not exactly what Joy was trying to tell the woman. Marie was drawing her own conclusions with a happily ever after. But a harder heart than Joy's would have to remove the hopeful smile from Marie's face.

"Your aunt is crazy," said Logan as soon as Joy got out of the car.

She patted his cheek. "Crazy smart, maybe. Crazy eccentric and exuberant…I'll buy that, too. Can she drive you crazy? Yup. But plain old crazy…not so much." She opened the back door, and Logan helped Bonnie get out of the car seat.

"Did you have a good visit?" he asked, stooping to her eye level.

"Yes. I gave out apples to everyone. Grandma only had two left. She said I should tell you congratulations on winning Joy."

"She did, did she? Well, thank you. I won the best prize of all, and I'm very happy. Want a piggyback ride to celebrate?" He hoisted her around to his back and took off down the driveway, Bonnie's giggles echoing in the air.

Joy followed more slowly and entered Logan's place through the kitchen door, where her aunt stood busily at the stove. Honey, still dressed to the nines and wearing high heels but coaxing the most delicious aromas from her dinner preparations. Garlic, spices, tomato sauce. Joy's salivary glands started working overtime.

Bart was setting the table. Bart?

"I could have handled supper," said Joy. "What happened to your dinner date?"

"Honey decided we didn't have an Italian restaurant in town. So here we are. Chicken cacciatore." He put his palms up and shrugged. "Wouldn't even consider The Lobster Pot." He stepped closer to Joy. "Don't tell your aunt I said this," he joked, "but she's a woman who knows her own mind."

And who managed to avoid meeting Bart's daughters and getting mixed up with his family. "My aunt is a very independent lady," said Joy, "and an excellent cook." She peeked into the skillet and inhaled. "Oh, that smells so good."

"Thank you, darling. I love feeding my family."

"Me, too? 'Cause I'm not your family." Bonnie had made her way next to Joy.

"Well, of course you are, little darling. You're living in this big house with Joy, aren't you?"

"Yes, yes." She leaned against her teacher. Automatically, Joy's arm went around her. Bonnie looked at Aunt Honey, then up at Joy. "You're both the same."

"We are?" asked Joy, mentally noting the differences in height, coloring, age. Honey was older than Daisy.

"In what way, Bonnie?" Logan had been listening from afar but now walked toward the ladies. "In what way are these two ladies the same?"

The child tilted her head back to see him. "They both make people happy." She hid her face against Joy.

Joy blinked rapidly. Logan said nothing. Honey stared at the girl she'd met only one day earlier. It was Bart who finally said, "And you're just like them, little lassie. You make people happy, too."

Bonnie turned around and shook her head. "Only Grandma. I only make Grandma happy."

"And me," said Joy. "You make me very happy." She kissed her on top of her curls.

She felt Logan's eyes on her and wasn't surprised when he approached. "Careful, sweetheart," he whispered. "You're moving into dangerous territory. Bonnie has a home. But more importantly, we're not ready." He nuzzled her neck. "I'd like you to myself for a while."

She loved that idea and couldn't wait to start her new life with Logan right here in this town. They hadn't spoken much about such practical matters, but she hadn't worried about them. Every minute was so jam-packed, she'd been living in the present, trying to handle each day as it came. She stared at Logan.

"I'd like that, too. I'm hoping we can plant roots in Pilgrim Cove. It's a perfect place to call home."

His arms came around her, and he glanced over his shoulder at Bart. "You heard the lady. Start finding a bigger house. I can work from home anywhere, but when I travel, I'll like the idea of her being surrounded by friends."

Bart slapped his hand on the table. "I knew it! I knew it. My instincts haven't failed me yet."

"One more thing," said Joy. "Can you work a little faster on this search than on my other one?"

Bart roared with laughter until tears ran. "Lassie, lassie. I work as fast or slow as needed. Each case is different."

Honey lowered the flame on the stove, walked to the table, and collapsed on the seat next to Bart. "Why, you old rascal. You set them up!"

Bart glanced at the ceiling, then, seeming to come to a decision, turned to his newest friend. "Well, Honeybelle, somebody has to do it. These young people waste too much time."

Joy's aunt took a moment. "So do not-so-young people. Which is why I've closed the gallery for the winter and am heading to Florida. It's time to have fewer responsibilities and more fun. But…before I leave, I want to see your work"—she pointed at Logan—"and see if my brother-in-law knows what he's talking about."

"Not necessary," said Logan.

"I'm sure it's not, from your point of view. You've established your credentials—"

"And I'm not looking for a gallery…never thought of it."

"However, discovering new artists is what I do," continued Honey, ignoring Logan's interruption. "It makes my heart race and my legs dance."

Joy watched her aunt smile sweetly. But her eyes—those blue eyes that Joy had inherited—gleamed with anticipation. Aunt Honey was definitely on a mission.

"So, Logan, please make Joy's favorite relative happy, and show me what you've got."

He glanced at Joy, a question on his face. "She knows her stuff," said Joy, "but it's totally up to you."

Logan had nothing to lose. If it worked out, he'd earn a little more for them to enjoy. If it didn't, so what? But first, he'd have a little fun with this tornado of a woman. Maybe spin Bart's head around, too.

He leaned over Joy's aunt where she sat at the table. "Honeybelle," he said softly, "are you asking to see my etchings?"

She jumped to her feet; her eyes gleamed. "You bet I am!" She paused. "Although that's such a cliché."

So the joke was on him. "Nice job, Honey."

"You have to rise before the early worm to put one over on my aunt," said Joy.

"Don't scare him, Joyful, because he's a keeper. You've picked a winner."

Maybe being part of a big family wouldn't be too bad.

CHAPTER THIRTEEN

"I'm not a princess, Logan. I'm the good witch from Oz. See my magic wand?" Bonnie twirled and waved her precious possession.

"What was I thinking?" He slapped his forehead in mock dismay. "You look exactly like a good witch."

"A fat good witch." She wrinkled her nose. "Ms. Joy said I had to wear a jacket underneath." Bonnie waved the wand at her three subjects. "Jax, you are now my brave lion. Here is your crown. I made it myself."

Logan bent down to the dog while Bonnie positioned the headgear, tying a ribbon under the dog's neck. "Just go along with it, boy," he whispered. "It's only for an hour."

The child beamed. "Abracadabra, let's go trick-or-treating."

"Have fun," said Joy, handing her the pumpkin-decorated tote bag they'd created together. "I'll stay home and hand out the candy…but first, some pictures. Give me your camera, please." She held out her hand for the camera strapped to Logan's body.

"I'll take them," he said.

"Not this time. I want to collect this memory—you guys together."

Two minutes later, the trick-or-treaters were off to explore the night and reap a traditional harvest of goodies. Front lights were ablaze at every house; street lamps helped illuminate the way, and flashlights bobbed in the hands of the walkers.

It was the first Halloween celebration of Logan's life. If he hadn't had the responsibility of caring for Bonnie, Logan would have taken pictures nonstop. The costumed kids, the dressed-up porches, some with scarecrows, most with giant pumpkins lit from inside, reminded him of a Norman Rockwell scene. Authentic small-town Americana. And so unlike anything he remembered from childhood.

He held Bonnie's hand as they crossed the street. She didn't let go on the other side, not even when they approached the first house.

"I'm scared," she said, stopping in mid-stride to look up at him. "What if they don't like me?"

His throat closed, and he swallowed hard. A familiar question. He'd been down that road a million times before he was ten years old. *What if they don't like me?*

"They're waiting for you, sweetheart. Just knock on the door and say trick or treat, and I guarantee whoever lives here will put candy in your pumpkin bag."

She pulled him forward. "Come with me, Logan."

"You bet."

A minute later, a happy Bonnie skipped back to the sidewalk with him, and Logan breathed a sigh of relief.

"Hey, Logan!"

He pivoted to see Adam and Sara, with her pal, Katie, and a man Logan assumed was her dad.

"Can Bonnie come with us to the next house?" asked Sara.

His little one looked excited at being with the older girls yet didn't leave his side. "What do you think, Bon? I'll be right here with Jax."

"Okay." She walked to Sara and reached for her hand. Looped the tote over her arm, and reached for Katie with her other hand. "Good."

"I see you pulled father duty tonight," said Adam, making introductions before Logan could protest his word choice. "Jason Parker, meet Logan Nash, who's staying in Sea View House temporarily."

The man's grin was engaging. "I know how that goes."

"Jason's headlining the Boston Fund concert at Christmas time," said Adam, "to support the bombing victims."

Jason Parker. The name sounded familiar. Jason... Not *that* Jason Parker? Songwriter, singer, platinum records... Logan held out his hand. "Glad to meet you."

His mind raced. What was that breakout song, the first hit? Something about Lila at the water's edge. Geez. How many Lilas could there be? The song had to be about Bart's granddaughter.

"I'm adding Luis Torres to headline with me," said Jason as though familiarity with the A-list of music talent was an ordinary subject anyone might have. "Luis thinks he's paying me back. But without him performing my songs in the beginning, I'd be nowhere."

"And I'm grateful for everything you and he do," said Adam. "Since Rebecca got hurt in the bombing, she's worked tirelessly to regain her strength and balance."

Logan looked from one to the other. Ordinary guys, with confidence to spare. He liked them. They seemed to accept him. Maybe he'd change his mind and read that journal Bart had left at the house. Maybe he'd understand this small town a bit better.

145

"I think you're all part of why Joy is happy here," said Logan. "She calls Pilgrim Cove home despite having a huge family who'd love her to move closer to them." The thought gave him a stomach ache. "If I can do anything to help out with the concert, let me know."

Jason cocked his head. "You beat me to it. I heard you were pretty good with a camera?"

"Seem to be."

"I'm thinking some publicity shots."

"No problem. I can manipulate a shot of Torres if you want one with the two of you together." He scanned the street. "Where are the girls?"

Without waiting for an answer, he unleashed the dog. "Find Bonnie, Jax. Find Bonnie." He pointed in the direction the girls had gone. Jax took off. And so did he, the other two men running at his side.

"They can't get lost," Jason said.

"They know to wait at corners."

"If anything happens to Bonnie, I'm a dead man. I may have pulled daddy duty tonight, but I'm not her dad. I'm not anyone's dad. And I'm not ready to be one. Look—I-I almost lost her. Lucky I have a wingman with a good nose."

The girls called to them as they drew closer, their voices coming from the walkway of a far house. Jax had them corralled. Logan whistled and Jax bounded to him. Bonnie followed, running right to Logan, arms up. "Look, look, Logan. Everyone gave me candy."

He lifted her, swung her around, and held her against his chest. "Fantastic. But don't walk so far ahead of me again. I couldn't see you. I was scared."

"Okay." She waved her wand. "We'll stay on the yellow brick road." She kissed his cheek and squirmed in his arms. "Down."

"Yes, ma'am."

So far, so good. He thought back and realized that this night was the first time he'd ever taken care of Bonnie by himself. He wasn't relaxed. He worried too much. He wasn't ready for this.

"No one's ever ready to be a dad."

He snapped toward Jason. "Are you a mind reader, too?"

The man laughed. "Don't have to be. It's all over your face—the fear, uncertainty. I know exactly where you're coming from. Katie was nine years old when I met her for the first time. I knew nothing about kids. Still figuring it out actually, now with a new baby."

Logan renewed his vow to read the journal. "Glad everything's working out."

"I did what I had to do." Jason wiped his forehead with an exaggerated motion. "Whew! Love's hard to figure out despite some of the sweet songs. It takes real work to find home. But…it's so worth it." His voice dropped to a conspiratorial whisper.

"No argument there," said Logan. "After more foster placements than I can remember, I'm finally looking at home." He could picture his and Joy's life together. Just the two of them, loving each other, counting on each other. Best friends till the end of their days. "Joy is…she's…incredible."

Adam slapped him on the back and glanced at Jason. "He's got it bad."

"Don't we all." He turned to Logan. "And don't do anything to screw it up."

Excellent advice. He intended to follow it.

##

Whether it was too much candy or too late a night for her kindergartners, the morning after Halloween proved to be a challenge. Two children cried; two others fell asleep. When noon came and the class disappeared to the lunchroom, Joy breathed a sigh of relief and chose to remain at her desk. She'd use her time to eat and re-energize for the afternoon session. Maybe start with an unusual activity—a nap.

She'd just picked up her sandwich when her cell phone rang. Marie Oakley.

"I need to speak with you alone," said Marie. "Can you visit without Bonnie?"

"What? Without Bonnie?"

"Yes. I'm afraid so."

Another setback? "Marie, tell the truth. Are you not healing properly?"

"I'm fine. It's th-the social worker. I have to talk to you."

Uh-oh. She didn't want to impose on Logan to babysit. He'd done a great job the prior evening, and that was enough. Her arrangement concerning Bonnie was just between Marie and herself. "It'll have to be on Monday during my lunch hour."

"I suppose that will do," said Marie. "But the sooner the better."

"I'll bring Bonnie to see you on Sunday. How's that?"

"Wonderful, but we can't talk then."

"I understand." She hung up with an ache in her heart. Marie was a rational woman and not one to jump to conclusions. Whatever the issue, Joy hoped she could help Marie solve it in a rational way.

On Monday, after a weekend of visits to the library, Grandma, and the grocery store, after acknowledging that her life and Logan's really did center around a five-year-old—delightful but demanding—and realizing that most young couples began differently, Joy ran through the doors of the rehab center at ten past noon.

Marie was waiting for her, her arm cast-free. "Let's go to my room, where there's privacy." She told Joy the number. "Would you mind pushing my wheelchair so I don't need an attendant?"

Once in her room, Marie lost no time talking. "Do you realize that your sixty-day guardianship is up next week? I cannot take care of Bonnie yet. A-and I don't know if I ever will be able to." She rubbed her eyes. "But we mustn't say anything like that to the social worker."

She pressed Marie's hand. "Maybe the woman can find you some help."

"Oh, she can make plans for me. In her assessment, she'll recommend lots of services available for the blind. But what about Bonnie? She keeps asking me if I've made arrangements for her. As if she were furniture I had to get rid of."

"Oh, my goodness."

"I have nobody, Joy. No nieces or nephews. Bonnie's mother was my only child. I loved her so much, and now her little one needs me. And I'm afraid…so afraid…"

"But no one can take Bonnie from you. You're her real legal guardian."

"But am I fit to be her mother, to act like a mother?" She wiped her eyes and sighed. "Just look at me now."

Joy remembered a conversation with her principal about Mrs. Cohen's mother. It was the children who ran to their blind mother's aid. Not vice versa. Mrs. Cohen couldn't imagine her mom taking care of a child on her own. Impossible. Yet Marie had done it—and although she may have worried, she'd never complained. Or asked for help. So far.

Marie squeezed Joy's hand tighter. "I need to come up with a plan. Bonnie needs a home, Joy, so I'm asking you…"

"But I can't answer, Marie. I love Bonnie, but I've got Logan to consider also, and he…"

"Joy! I know what the social worker has in mind. Bonnie will go into the foster care system, where kids fall between the cracks. And what will happen to our Bonnie then?"

Our Bonnie. Oh, God. What a situation. Maybe they could extend the guardianship period. But those days would pass, too, and then what?

"I've had nothing to do but think," Marie said. "Testing out dozens of scenarios, but only one makes sense. A permanent home with people who love her."

"You're right," Joy whispered. "I'll do it." *And pray Logan understands.*

It was cold outside on the deck, much too cold for a simple conversation, but Joy had insisted on bringing him outside. "For privacy," she'd said, nodding toward the bedroom Bonnie slept in.

And then she dropped the bomb.

"You told Marie what? Forever?" He couldn't believe she'd made a promise like that. "This is a big deal. Didn't you think we should talk it over first?"

Disappointment flowed through him. Then anger arrived. "I thought we were a team. I thought we would share. That's what you said so many times."

"And I meant it."

But it wasn't true. When reality had reared its head, she'd done what she wanted with no thought of him. She'd chosen the child without thinking of consequences.

Bonnie was a great kid. But now he knew, if Joy let him down, he couldn't count on anyone. Ever. What was the point?

She stood in front of him, her arms on his waist. "Please, Logan. Please, listen. I love you. I love you so much it hurts. We are a team. We have been a team. And I'm not walking away." Now she put her bare hands on his cheeks.

"Logan," she whispered. "I told Marie I had to talk to you first, but remember the social worker who's been managing her case?"

He'd heard about her and nodded.

"She's already determined that Marie can't handle Bonnie anymore. Maybe it has a bad rap, but I didn't think the foster care system was right for—"

"Foster Care!" he shouted when he wanted to howl. "Not that. Not our Bonnie. No, no, and never."

He pulled back from her and started to pace. "Know how many times I ran away? Know how many people take you in just for the money? And treat you like a thing and not a person. Like you owe them the ground they walk on? Know how many drink too much?"

Maybe he'd just been unlucky. Maybe there were good, decent couples out there with hearts. "Even if I were just unlucky, if the system's getting a bad rap, maybe there's fire beyond the smoke."

"So…so what are you saying, Logan?" she asked, standing before him, hope in her eyes but one hand over the other, twisting the ring around her finger.

He pressed his large hands over her smaller ones, stilling them. "I'm saying I'm an ass. You did the right thing. You're strong, unafraid, and know what's important." He gathered her close. "I love you so much, Joy. You're just perfect."

She did the eye roll thing. "Only my dad would agree with you."

He started to laugh. "Well, you're perfect for me! But you'd better let them know that their family is expanding again."

"After we check it out with Bonnie. She may be very young, but she understands a lot."

CHAPTER FOURTEEN

Six weeks later in Sea View House

"Once upon a time, there was a handsome prince who always carried a magic picture box with him. He also had a trusty steed at his side." Bonnie sat on the floor with her two new cousins and leaned closer to them. "A steed's really a horse," she explained, "but in this story it's a big dog. Okay?"

The boys nodded, and Joy put her hand on her mouth to hold back her giggles. Logan guided her away from Bonnie's line of vision. "Shh," he whispered. "Let's listen to this."

"But the prince was sad because he had no friends." Bonnie sighed dramatically and shrugged with despair. "Very sad, but"—she brightened up—"one day he met a beautiful princess who looked like a butterfly."

"Aww…that's stupid."

"No, it's not! The princess was decorated in a million colors and hopped from place to place, always having fun. One day, she went on a hunt and found a little girl. Her name was Bon-Bon. And the princess took Bon-Bon home."

Joy put her mouth to Logan's ear. "You've got to write this down. It's priceless, and she'll want it when she grows up."

He nodded toward Chance, who was taking a video. "Even better."

"When the prince saw the princess with the little girl, he was so happy. He said, 'Will you both marry me and be my family?'"

She looked up then, spotted Logan, and ran to him. "Right, Daddy?"

"Right." He picked her up and twirled her around. "A perfect story."

From high in her dad's arms, Bonnie reached for Joy. "Right?"

"Oh, yes, sweetheart. You got it just right."

"Here, here!" proclaimed Mac. "Champagne for everyone, and a toast to my newest grandchild and her terrific parents. Joy…you live right here," he said, patting his heart. "And Logan…you're all right. Little Bonnie picked herself a great daddy. I suppose her grandma Marie would say, all's well that ends well, and she'd be right. And for that, I welcome Marie into our family, too.

"And a toast to Pilgrim Cove. A great place to call home—and not too far from us!"

"This is a first!" said Bart Quinn. "A winter wedding at Sea View House. And a new family at the same time." He turned to his old friends and his new one, who'd flown back from Florida for the event. "I really think I've outdone myself with this one."

"That you have." Sam Parker, Doc Rosen, Rick O'Brien surrounded him with congratulations on yet another bit of magic.

"I wouldn't know," said Honeybelle. "You'll have to ask me in ten years."

"A bit of a cynic, are ya?"

She raised her wine glass. "A toast to the happy couple. May the wind be always at their back."

Perfunctory, thought Bart, but six glasses joined hers. "Amen. *L'chaim. Salud.*"

"Not only the wind but the mighty Atlantic, the sand, and the gulls. That's a fact for you to mull over." He had their attention now. Even Honey looked interested. "They're planting their roots, ya see, and put a down payment on Butterfly Cottage."

"Butterfly Cottage?" said Rick. "It's a beauty, but it's huge. The name is misleading."

"Not to our besotted groom. As soon as he heard the name, he wanted to buy it for Joy. And after the excellent inspection…there was no stopping him. Must have taken every penny he'd saved." He looked innocently at the ceiling. "I wonder why he'd do something like that." He turned to Honey and answered his own question. "It's called love, my dear. Love."

Honey wrinkled her nose. "Practicality. They needed enough room for the MacKenzies to visit."

Stubborn woman. Bart pointed at Sam. "Have they spoken with you and Matt about the remodel? They want Marie with them, but in her own apartment where she can relax and be her own boss. She's taking on the construction expense. I've already had two lookers for her current house. One is coming back."

He gestured toward the bride and groom. "Take a picture of that."

Honey bit her lip and gazed across the room at the celebratory couple. Logan's arm gently encircled Joy as they moved through the crowd. His eyes adored her. She watched Joy rise on tiptoe and deliver a kiss on his cheek, her eyes shining with love.

At that moment, Bonnie ran to them, arms raised high. "Mommy, Daddy, me, too. Me, too." They raised her between them. Kisses and laughter all around.

Bart turned to Honey again. "What do you say now?"

"I will quote from the newest member of my family, who's a very wise child. 'And they lived happily ever after.'"

SEA VIEW HOUSE JOURNAL

(Pilgrim Cove Series)

From Laura McCloud Parker—I arrived at Sea View House in March, looking for a place to catch my breath and get on with life. I'd just lost my mom and completed my own breast cancer treatment, one event right after the other. The first person I met in Pilgrim Cove, besides Bart Quinn, was Matt Parker. And the first part of him I saw was his jeans and work boots, sticking out from beneath my kitchen sink. "Hand me the wrench," he said, thinking I was his son. How could I have known then that living in this *House on the Beach* would forever change my life? Bart says it's a magical place. I'm not arguing.....

From Shelley Anderson Stone—The children and I arrived at Sea View House on Memorial Day weekend. Divorce hurts everybody, and we all needed time to recover. Bart Quinn had given us the large apartment downstairs called the Captain's Quarters. I had no idea that Daniel Stone would be living upstairs in the Crow's Nest, dealing with his own grief. I also had no idea he would rock my world—in the very best of ways—and that we'd provide each other with a second chance at love. Looking back, I can say that season was *No Ordinary Summer* for any of us....

From Daniel Stone—Read Shelley's account. Here's my P.S.: If there's any magic at all, it was provided by Jesse, my golden retriever. Two little kids and a golden? Pure magic.

From Rachel Goodman Levine—Like a prodigal daughter, I returned to my hometown of Pilgrim Cove in the fall, trying to prove myself as an assistant principal of the high school. Instead of living with my folks, I landed at Sea View House. I wasn't alone there. Thank you, Bart Quinn! Marine biologist Jack Levine had settled into the Crow's Nest. My initial delight turned to dismay when Jack joined my teaching staff, breaking all the rules with his unorthodox methods. And getting me into trouble. It was then the magic happened. The discovery. The love. Somehow, we *Reluctant Housemates* are now housemates forever right here in Pilgrim Cove....

From Jack Levine—Read Rachel's story. All I'll say is: magic, my eye! Sure, I'll admit that sailors are a superstitious bunch. But here's what really happened: My boat went missing and shook her up. It wasn't magic. It was a miracle! All of it. So believe what you want.

 From Jason Parker—I came back after nine years because I couldn't outrun the pain. Prom night. A car wreck. My twin brother gone. Our music gone with him. Except not. I've got platinum behind me, and what does it mean? Nothing without the folks I love. Less than nothing without Lila Sullivan. She's always been the one, the only one for me. Bless Bart Quinn for lending me Sea View House. My daughter was conceived there a long time ago. But I didn't know anything about her all those years. Folks might call Katie *The Daughter He Never Knew*, and they'd be right. But I know her now. As for her mom and me…? Sea View House came through for us again. Our wedding took place right there. I believe in the magic. I believe in happily ever after. If that's not love, what is?

From Lila Sullivan Parker—Read Jason's account. All I'll add is that the right girl for lovely Adam Fielding is still out there. Jason's return saved Adam and me from a tepid marriage of convenience. We both deserved more. My money's on Adam and Sea View House.

(Sea View House Series)

From Rebecca Hart Fielding—It's summer again, a year since the last entry in this journal. The magic is still here. In this place, in this town, in its people. After the Boston Marathon, I arrived at Sea View House with no expectations except to focus on rehab. I wanted to hide, but that's impossible in Pilgrim Cove. In a nutshell, I met Adam in a bar. A nice bar at The Wayside Inn. It was definitely *not* love at first sight. But something changed along the way.

From Adam Fielding—We fell in love. That's what happened. That's the magic everyone talks about. No woo-woo. No smoke and mirrors. Scientists don't believe in that stuff. When Becca came to Sea View House, all she wanted to do was walk again. She was stubborn. She was proud. And she was determined to remain the athlete she'd always been. I'm happy to say that *Her Long Walk Home* brought her straight into my arms.

From Joy MacKenzie Nash – If anyone needed the magic of Sea View House, it was Logan and me. He didn't believe in it, of course. But grief lived in my heart, and I was open to anything. How ironic that this kindergarten teacher couldn't have her own children. I pretended to be happy. Maybe I overdid the act. When Logan met me, he thought I was a ditz, and I thought he was the loneliest person I'd ever met, always hiding behind his camera.

From Logan Nash – Love stared at me through the lens of my Nikon. Joy, Joy, Joy. She was everywhere. But what I did I know about love? Nothing. I was a foster care kid, never dreaming of a family of my own, not even knowing how an ordinary family worked. And the magic? When Joy said yes, her eyes shining with love, I knew that between us, she'd get *Her Picture-Perfect Family*. And so would I. That's magic enough for me.

EXCERPT FROM
MUSIC OF THE NIGHT
(SEA VIEW HOUSE SERIES BOOK THREE)

PROLOGUE

Pilgrim Cove, December 2012

The threat of snow and his flaring arthritis didn't stop Bart Quinn from bringing a huge welcome basket from Quinn Realty and Property Management to Alison Berg, the newest permanent resident of Pilgrim Cove. His partner and granddaughter, Lila, had worked closely with him on this assignment.

The young widow from Boston, had given them a punch list of criteria, beginning with safety. No house with beach or bay access. Her baby son had started walking and would want to explore. Too dangerous. Much too dangerous. As were busy streets and cars. Could he find a quiet area? He and Lila had done their best, but the more private, the more expensive. Alison couldn't afford that luxury.

He exited his old reliable Town Car, reached for the gift and waited for Lila to join him from her own vehicle.

"Glad you're with me, today," he said, as they walked toward the second house from the corner on Neptune Street. "Alison needs to make friends her own age."

"Maybe. But don't push her, Granddad. She needs to find her way."

"I never push, darling. I just…uh…

"Manipulate? Arrange? I love you dearly, but I've been around you a long time, and know exactly how you work!"

Bart chuckled. His lassie was right. He glanced from Alison's house across the street to where the Romanos lived. Father and son. Just perfect. Mike Romano was exactly what Alison Berg needed…in time. In a little more time.

They rang the bell.

##

At the sound of the doorbell, her baby boy crawled faster than Alison walked, despite the cartons and boxes littering the floor. She ran to Joey, scooped him up, and grabbed a light blanket. "Peek-a-boo," she crooned while draping it over him. She had to protect him from the cold, especially his head. Wasn't that in the baby books?

When she spotted Bart and Lila through the sidelight, she opened the door and smiled. "Welcome to my mess."

"We won't stay but a minute," said Lila, closing the door behind her. "Just wanted to bring some sunshine on a gray winter day." She took the basket from Bart but addressed Alison. "Your arms are full. Where…?

"Probably on the dining room table. It's a beautiful bouquet. Thank you."

"Welcome to Pilgrim Cove," said Bart. "Now let's see who's hiding under that blanket." He pulled the covering off. "Peek-a-boo!"

The child squealed with delight and bounced in his mother's arms.

"He is so adorable," said Lila, grinning, "and look at that hair, like burnished copper. Yours is just a bit darker, but mother and son are unmistakable."

"You should have seen his father. Spitting image except for the hair." She'd heard the comparison often. Redheads were the rare breed, and Joey and she were a match. But that left Peter out of the conversation. *Oh, Peter. What you are missing.*

She blinked away tears that still came too easily. Not even unexpected guests could distract her enough. But she tried to smile as she led them further inside.

"Thank you so much. Not only flowers but cookies, candy…." The basket held a full array of temptation.

"A small token to say you're not alone," said Bart. "New to town? Aye. But you've got friends, lassie. Right here."

The man reminded Alison of her dad. He also reminded her of Pete. Big men. Blustering men. Loving hard and spewing reassurances as if they could protect all in their care. But who protected them?

"I'll be fine as long as Joey is happy. And safe." She kissed the baby on the cheek and bounced him in her arms. "No more big cities. Ever again."

The ensuing silence was broken by Lila. "I grew up in Pilgrim Cove, fell in love here, and had heartache here, too. But it worked out." She patted her stomach. "You can't tell much yet, but Jason and I are expecting at the end of May. Our second."

"It's the magic," said Bart. "And you've been sprinkled with it, too, my dear Alison. You stayed in Sea View House last June and came back to stay for good."

Mr. Quinn was quite the character. Magic? More like black magic.

"Granddad, enough drama!" Lila rolled her eyes. "What I'm trying to say, Alison, is that we're a good town, but we're not Shangra La. We're real people. Just like anywhere else."

Alison had liked Lila Parker from the beginning of the house hunting experience. Open and honest. Maybe they'd become real friends. "I've done my research," said Alison. "Crime is low here. Schools are good. Joey's grandparents are all in Boston, which is a manageable ride, and that's good enough for me."

"Ah, then they'll be sure to come down for Christmas," said Bart.

Without Peter? No. No holidays this year. No Christmas. No Hanukkah. No nothing. But her decision was nobody's business. She shrugged. "We'll see."

"The ROMEOs are all in town," said Bart, extracting a business card from his inside coat pocket. "No one's run south for the winter. So if you need anything at all, have questions, want a referral…you can count on us. We know everyone."

Alison took the card listing Bart's buddies, all Retired Old Men Eating Out, with phone numbers and specialties. "If I need an electrician, I'll call Ralph Bigelow. But right now, I need a pediatrician, and I don't think the ROMEOs have the answer!"

"But I do," said Lila. "Actually Doc Rosen, who's on that list, recommended her years ago, and we've all been very happy, including my ten year old daughter, Katie." She scrambled through her purse for pencil and paper. "Here you go." Turning toward the door, she said, "And now we'll leave you to unpack in peace."

Alison saw the instant Lila spotted the cello case lying on its side. Saw the interest illuminating the woman's face. Knew she'd be asking questions, and her own stomach tensed. She had to cut the conversation off before it began.

"I haven't played it in a very long time." With a casual wave of her hand, she added, "maybe I'll give it away." As if. The instrument had been a gift. A three hundred year old Italian crafted gift worth more than the heavily mortgaged house she'd just bought. She hoped, however, that she'd diminished Lila's interest.

"Wow. If you really mean that, please keep me in mind. The kids in my family are incredibly talented. Another instrument would be a happy challenge for them." She stepped closer and grinned. "As my husband has learned and now says, 'talent is not to be trifled with'."

A shiver ran through Alison. Echoes from the past. *Nurture the gift.* Lila's husband must be the real deal. Her mind raced through the Boston area musicians she knew, relieved not to recognize the name Parker. She was starting a new life. "I-I'm sorry…?"

"Jason. Jason Parker."

It took her a moment. Then knew her suspicions were confirmed. Lila's husband was the real deal. All over the pop charts, composer, singer, performer. A piano man. Thank God their lives wouldn't cross musically. Maybe she'd rethink a friendship with Lila.

The bell rang again just as Alison and her guests reached the door. She pulled it open, looked up, a long way up past the scruffy beard, and stared into the bluest eyes she'd ever seen.

"Mike Romano," he said, thrusting a package at her, "from across the street." A delicious aroma emanated from the bag. "It's shepherd pie. My dad likes to cook, and you probably need some supper." He stared at her, then glanced at the others. "The snow's started, and we're going to have some wicked weather. You'd better get on home. Want me to drive you, Bart?"

The older man glared. "Ask me again in twenty years, boyo."

Romano smiled, a sweet, crooked, one-side-of-his-mouth smile, and a corner of Alison's heart tore. So familiar.

"Thank you, and thank your dad," she said, now watching her other guests walk to their vehicles. Romano hadn't lied. The snow was starting to fall in serious fashion.

"Here's my business card, Red. The home number's on it. If you lose electricity or need anything, give us a call."

Joey had fallen asleep in her arms, and she gave him a kiss. "I've got to put him down, he's getting heavier every day." She placed the baby carefully in his porta-crib and once more turned to her neighbor.

"My name's Alison. Don't call me Red or Lucy or carrot top."

Mike Romano's attention traveled from the baby to her. "My hearing's not too good, Red. But I come in handy from time to time."

If he was trying to be funny, he'd failed. "I'm not laughing, Mr. Romano." She looked at his card. *Romano Landscape and Design*. "Nice. So are you on vacation all winter?"

That crooked grin appeared again. "If you call street plowing a vacation…volunteer firefighting… and swimming coach at the Y…and planning landscape designs for clients for spring installation. We cut and trim trees for the county in our spare time."

Impressive. "You handle everything but the kitchen sink."

He winked. "For that you call a plumber."

She burst out laughing. It was the weirdest thing, the juxtaposition of her and the baby in a god-awful messy house, talking with a bunch of strangers, and a guy calling her Red. Nothing made sense. Especially her giggles.

Nerves. Stress. Relieved by a lame joke. Mike Romano's stupid joke.

"I think you've broken the spell," she gasped. "I haven't laughed since my husband died."

He rubbed the back of his neck. "Yeah. I-I'm sorry for your loss. But not for the laughter. They say it's the best medicine."

"A cliché, but maybe…" She shrugged.

Mike scanned the house, left and right, and behind Alison. "Looks like you've got a load of work ahead. So I'll let you at it." He opened the door. "Got my number, just in case?"

Oh, she had his number. A born flirt with a sense of humor hard to ignore. Probably picked up women wherever he went. At least, she didn't have to deal with that. She held up his business card. "Got it."

He waved and closed the door behind him.

She glanced at her son, then at the door. "He couldn't get away fast enough. So who's the real baby?" Shrugging, she made her way to the kitchen and began to unpack.

Mr. Blue Eyes didn't matter. Her music didn't matter. She'd resigned her position from the South Shore Philharmonic. Nothing mattered anymore. Except little Joey.

HELLO FROM LINDA

Dear Reader:

Thank you so much for choosing to read ***Her Picture-Perfect Family***. I hope you enjoyed your visit to Pilgrim Cove and the second story in my new *Sea View House* series. For some of you, ***Her Picture-Perfect Family*** was an introduction to this cozy beach town. For others, it was a reunion with old friends from the *Pilgrim Cove* series. In either case, I hope the story kept you turning the pages as Joy MacKenzie and Logan Nash found their way home together by following their hearts.

If you enjoyed this book, please help others find it so they can discover Linda Barrett books, too. Here's what you can do:

• Write an honest review and post it on Amazon, Barnes & Noble, iBooks, GoodReads or any of your favorite book sites
• Keep up with me at my website at *www.linda-barrett.com* to find out about upcoming books and what's going on in the writing world
• Sign up for my newsletter at *http://lindabarrett.authornewsletters.com/?p=su bscribe&id=3*
• Join me on Facebook at: *https://www.facebook.com/linda.barrett.353*
• Tell your friends! The best book recommendations come from friends because we trust them.

I truly appreciate your help in getting the word out about ***Her Picture-Perfect Family*** and my other novels, which are listed here and available electronically and in print.

Many thanks,
Linda

LINDA BARRETT BOOKS

NOVELS—ROMANCE:

(Sea View House Series)
Her Long Walk Home, 2015 (Bk. 1)
Her Picture-Perfect Family, 2015 (Bk. 2)

(Harlequin Books, Superromance)
Quarterback Daddy, 2010
Summer at the Lake, 2009
Houseful of Strangers, 2007
A Man of Honor, 2006

(Pilgrim Cove Series - Harlequin Books)
The House on the Beach, 2004 (Bk. 1)
No Ordinary Summer, 2004 (Bk. 2)
Reluctant Housemates, 2005 (Bk. 3)
The Daughter He Never Knew, 2005 (Bk. 4)

The Inn at Oak Creek, 2003
The Apple Orchard, 2002
True-Blue Texan, 2001
Love, Money and Amanda Shaw, 2001

NOVELS—WOMEN'S FICTION:

The Soldier and the Rose, 2014
Family Interrupted, 2013

SHORT NOVELLA:

Man of the House, 2013 (part of *Celebrate Romance* anthology with four other authors)

MEMOIR:

HOPEFULLY EVER AFTER: Breast Cancer, Life and Me, 2013 (true story about surviving breast cancer twice)

Printed in Great Britain
by Amazon